The Springsweet

Other Books by Saundra Mitchell

The Vespertine

Shadowed Summer

The Springsweet

SAUNDRA MITCHELL

HARCOURT

Houghton Mifflin Harcourt

Boston   New York   2012

The lines of poetry on p. 135 are taken from "Goblin Market" by Christina Rossetti,
in *Goblin Market and Other Poems* (Macmillan & Co., 1862).
Those on p. 211 are paraphrased and taken from "Lord Randall" in *The English and Scottish
Popular Ballads* (Houghton Mifflin, 1882).

Harcourt is an imprint of Houghton Mifflin Harcourt Publishing Company.

www.hmhbooks.com

Text set in Cochin.

Library of Congress Cataloging-in-Publication Data
Mitchell, Saundra.
The springsweet / by Saundra Mitchell.
p. cm.
Companion book to: The Vespertine.
Summary: Moving from Baltimore to Oklahoma Territory in the late 1800s,
seventeen-year-old Zora experiences the joys and hardships of pioneer life,
discovering new love and her otherworldly power.
ISBN 978-0-547-60842-6 [1. Supernatural—Fiction. 2. Love—Fiction. 3. Frontier and
pioneer life—Oklahoma—Fiction. 4. Oklahoma—History—19th century—Fiction.] I.
Title.
PZ7.M6953Sp 2012
[Fic]—dc23

2011027319

Manufactured in the United States of America
DOC 10 9 8 7 6 5 4 3 2 1
4500346199

For Janie Beth, Jacob, and Cassy—
Remain thou as thou art.

One

That I went a little mad, I could not deny.

Those endless months in mourning clothes saved me and destroyed me; I got used to my own silence and to the delicate passing of footsteps. No one invited me to tea or to dance. They didn't even ask me to speak over cold dinners; often, I had the pleasure of eating alone.

After two months, I should have packed away my black dress, remembering death with just a dark ribbon in my hair. After six months, I should have taken callers and started at the new girls' High School. But I didn't, and I wouldn't — I remained cloaked in ebony satin, my steps slow, as if taken through an ocean of dreams.

I woke, I slept, and I waited, endlessly waited, for my Thomas Rea, who would never call on me again.

After a year, my mother decided to rip down my black crêpe by force.

"They're your friends," Mama said, brisk as always. "So I sent your card out."

I think she meant for me to argue, but what argument could I make? I was neither widow nor wife.

Freshly seventeen, I should have had roses in my cheeks and laughter in my heart. I should have savored the dawn of spring. But then, I shouldn't have known, to the drop, how much blood could spill from a boy before he turned gray and breathed no more.

Mama flipped her dough, leaning in hard to knead it. "You'll have Mattie and Victoria, and Grace if she's over that cold of hers. Hope she doesn't drag it in, anyway. She should know better."

Winding the paring knife round and round, I bared an apple's flesh. I had no reply.

"Thought I'd like to invite some badgers, too," Mama said, turning a grave look in my direction. "Maybe we'll strip to our corsets and have a parade in the park."

When I said nothing still, Mama made an ugly sound. Flipping the dough again, she banged from one end of the counter to the other. What she meant to do, I couldn't imagine. So when she snatched her pine rolling pin and pounded the table in front of me, I jumped.

The knife bit into my thumb.

"Oh, duck," Mama said, her voice strained as she wrapped her apron around my hand. "What did you do that for?"

I shook my head, watching scarlet blossom through white muslin. I had no tears for this ridiculous little wound.

"You're alive," she said, squeezing until my hand throbbed. Lifting it above my head, she tugged me to my feet. How peculiar it seemed that she didn't tower over me anymore.

"You're alive, Zora Stewart," she repeated, catching my chin with her unencumbered hand. "And you have to be alive until your time comes."

Rolling my gaze round to hers, I opened my mouth. Like the creaking of a neglected hinge, my voice came out slow and croaking. "Do you know what I dream?"

"Tell me."

"Every night, I drown in fire," I said. Numb, my lips barely shaped my words. "Endlessly, Mama. I drown in it, and the sky is as wide as the sea."

Opening the hot tap, Mama rinsed blood from my fingers. "There's neither heaven nor hell on this earth, but those you make."

"I made none of this."

"And yet you succumb."

"Arrange something for me, then," I said, reclaiming my hand.

"Arrange it yourself," Mama replied. "You'll take callers this week."

Drawn by habit, I touched the locket at my throat. It held my remembrance of Thomas, a single curl of his hair closed in a silver shell. I had made all my arrangements, and none would ever be. "I meant a match. A marriage. Just to have it done with."

Mama touched my chin, turning my face to hers. "One cage into another is no life at all."

But I had gone mad in those months. Just the littlest bit, and madness sometimes guises itself as reason. My fingers trailed from the locket, and likewise my gaze from Mama's. I took up my paring knife and apple, and made up my unsettled mind.

I would *not* dance, I decided. Go calling, play snapdragon, go riding in street cars—none of it. My merry days were over, my heart too broken to beat again. It was time to put away notions and games, childhood and hopes. My decision was made: I would be married.

But first, I needed counsel.

～～～～～

I walked down Fayette Street alone. As I wore black, no one bothered me—my destination was clear.

The Westminster Burying Ground sat in a small plot, penned on every side by a city growing in desperate gasps. I opened the iron gate and avoided the odd fellow standing there—one of the boys who appeared with cognac and two glasses: one for them, and one for Mr. Poe. They dissipated themselves intentionally, drinking to the memory of a drunk who'd died in a gutter.

I longed to throw rocks at them, to chase them away—to dare them to grieve just once over something real and then decide if it was romantic.

They, I think, considered me kindred. This one saw me and raised his glass. As if we could be the same—these fools who suffered intentionally, and I, who longed to sink into the ground with my love and sleep forevermore.

From my cloak, I pulled a horsehair brush. Skimming it across Thomas' marker, I cleaned the soft limestone. His martyr's arrow stood out in perfect relief; there would be no forgetting.

Guiltily, I polished his name, because I *had* begun to forget. When I clutched the locket round my throat, I couldn't remember whether the lock of his hair inside was more auburn or strawberry. I had an impression of his voice that had faded, as if called down a corridor.

The wind lifted, and speckled white petals fluttered around me, the gentlest snow. I murmured, "I'm thinking of sending away to be a farmer's wife, Thomas. In the Territories."

Quiet answered, but not silence. Instead of Thomas' voice, ships in the harbor cried their comings, their goings. Men worked nearby, singing as they laid mortar, and hoofbeats argued with the disconcerting hum of the streetcars.

"There are magazines full of them—widowers wanting wives to raise their motherless children."

From the corner of my eye, I saw Poe's Visitor finish his glass, and set the glass on the stone—no doubt to leave it there. The dead did not drink; they certainly didn't ruin their own burying yard. Living men did that—careless ones. Damping my ire, I turned my attention to Thomas again.

"Is it a bad idea? I don't think you'd mind, but I just don't know." Sinking slowly to my knees, I pressed my forehead against the limestone. How queer it felt—warm as flesh in the places it basked in the sun, and cool as water in the shadows.

Only the roughness of the stone, already weathered, answered me. A slow tide of grief filled me; I murmured, "I wish you'd say. I wish you'd haunt me, Thomas. You're so still."

Someone approached from behind; I stiffened and drank up my tears.

"Miss?"

Turning, I lifted my face to Poe's Visitor. He was carelessly handsome, his coat unbuttoned. Ink spotted his sleeves, accusing black specks on the cuffs. He reminded me overmuch of an artist, or an actor — so caught in his own head he couldn't behave, even in a graveyard.

Coolly, I asked, "Can I help you?"

He offered his hand and a concerned look. "That's what I meant to ask you."

Gathering myself, I wanted to rise up as my mother would. I wanted to be full and great, such a wall that none would trouble me. But my mother's voice wouldn't have quavered; mine did when I said, "Thank you, no."

Glancing at the stone, he asked, "A friend?"

"Hardly!" I bristled, then stopped short.

What could I say? I felt like a widow, but I wasn't. To call Thomas friend lied about everything we ever were. Angry tears stung my eyes again, and I ducked around this intruder. I owed him no explanation.

"You shouldn't walk home alone," Poe's Visitor called after me, but he chose not to follow.

Stealing a glance as I hurried through the gate, I saw that he'd already turned away. Hands folded, he considered the headstone instead of me, his dark hair overlong and fingered by the wind. Standing beneath a flowering pear, he cut a fine figure. Tall and straight, broad of shoulder — plainly kind.

And yet I felt nothing. No curiosity about his name or his provenance, no desire to write him into a dance card or take his hand in a darkened garden.

That had to be Thomas' answer.

If I couldn't imagine a life with anyone else, then I had to give myself to good intentions and hard work. Mothering in Kansas or the Territories or anyplace but Baltimore, Maryland, would do.

~~~~~

"It's not as though I'm complaining," Mattie complained, trying to balance her teacup and saucer on her knees, "but I thought we might catch up a bit over *tea*, not newspapers."

Victoria turned a page and made a funny noise. "I can read and catch up at the same time."

My gloves abandoned, I stood at the table, poring over the newspaper I'd claimed for my own. "You know my particulars — I'm the same as I ever was. How are you?"

"Distractible," Mattie said. She leaned over her cup to implore me. "My silver toilette's gone all ragged at the hems. I wanted to wear it to the Sugarcane Ball, and now I can't."

"How distressing," I said as I ran my finger along the paper. Passing inquiries for nurses and teachers and clerks, I skipped to the bottom of the page and lit up when I finally found my particular heading:

SITUATIONS OFFERED

Slowly, I sank into my seat, reading through the listings. Miners and land grabbers and cattlemen—they'd traveled west to find their fortunes but had to write back east to find their wives. So many asked for a cooing dove, a docile lamb, a darling kitten, that I wondered if I'd stumbled on inquiries for a zoo.

Mattie raised her cup. "Are you going to come?"

"Where?" I asked.

"The Sugarcane Ball," Mattie said. She gave a suffering sigh. "Are you paying attention at all?"

"I hardly am, I admit."

Victoria laughed under her breath, then closed her paper with a flourish. Propping elbows on the table, she shrugged. "It's all miners in this one."

"That won't do," I said.

"Why not?" Mattie opened her fan. She hid all but her eyes behind it, flapping it lazily. Then, with a snap, she closed it again. It was all practice for the ball, though she didn't need it. Her startling blue eyes needed no frame to improve them.

"Miners are dirty," Victoria said. She hesitated, then reached for the next paper. "And poor."

"They're *gold* miners, realize."

"It's gambling, realize."

"If it means a lovely house with running water upstairs and down, *and* a water closet, *and* a girl to come in every day, I have no philosophical objection to gambling," Mattie replied. She moved to snap her wrist, and I caught it. The rattle of fan bones had driven me to distraction.

"Just as like to end up in a shanty," I told her. "I'm looking for someone settled."

"Find someone here, at the *ball*," Mattie said. She turned her eyes up at me, making no move to reclaim her hand. Distinctly doll-like, she slid to the edge of her chair to plead. "Everyone's leaving me. Can't you stay?"

A scold flew to my lips. Our dear friends hadn't *left* us. Thomas and Sarah weren't traveling on holiday; Amelia and Nathaniel weren't simply *away*. These separations couldn't be cured with cards and reunions—they were dead. All dead: Thomas bled and Sarah poisoned; Nathaniel burned and Amelia fevered.

It was the last that broke me irreparably. Attending funeral upon funeral, and Caleb's disappearance before trial, was more than I wanted to bear. But bear it I did, thinking Mama would soon relent and bring Amelia back home to Baltimore. Instead came a letter.

Three spare lines in an unfamiliar hand informed us that Amelia had taken a fever on returning to Maine and expired forthwith. Her brother sent no memento; I had nothing but memories and despair. Thus, I commended myself to madness.

Our sixteenth summer lay buried—how could Mattie be so frivolous? Honestly, how could I? My mood's delicate bubble burst. I turned to the papers still spread on the table.

"What good is any of this, I wonder?" I asked.

A sudden wind filled the room, cool and almost wet with its freshness. But it was no balm; I panicked when I felt it. My mother's errands hadn't lasted nearly as long as I expected.

"Hurry," I said, scrambling to hide my papers and catalogs. "Put the cups and pot back on the table!"

"God save us from sailors! The harbor's teeming with them. Can't hardly go a step without . . ." Fingers poised at her temples, smoothing back loose curls, Mama narrowed her eyes at us. "This seems too precious by half."

I lifted my teacup, sipping at cold, sugared dregs. "You sent them my card, Mama. Of course, I invited them in."

Gliding into the parlor, Mama eyed the table, then smiled at Mattie. "How do you do, dear?"

"Very well, thank you," Mattie said, folding her hands neatly as doves in her lap. "It's been a lovely tea. I've even convinced Zora to come to the Sugarcane Ball."

Through gritted teeth, I said, "We had only considered it, Mattie."

Mama ignored the tone of my voice, refusing to see the hard cut of my eyes and how stiffly I sat. She heard what she wished to hear: I'd be a good girl again, worried about dresses and dances, the darkness of last summer finally put aside.

"Oh, Zora," Mama said, engulfing me in a powdery hug, "I couldn't be happier!"

Over Mama's shoulder, I caught a glimpse of my oldest but least dear friend. Mattie shone with a silvery, pristine smile. She'd gotten her way. I'd come out of mourning at the Sugarcane Ball—that she'd forced me meant nothing.

Two

"I'll mind your dance card," Mattie said, and took it directly from my hand.

My mother had given her a wildly inflated sense of her importance—*Mind her and make sure she dances,* she'd told her. Now Mattie had her own card to fill, and mine as well, the gossamer cord looped around her wrist to secure it. As if I might decide to scrap with her about it; as if it might actually come to blows.

And then, briefly, I considered it, for what a pretty way that would be to ruin both this new season of mine and the candied sweetness of Evergreen House's first public social.

Like a confection, the Sugarcane Ball devoted itself entirely to indulgence. Organza shimmered over the windows and streamed from valance to valance, all shades of white and cream to match the ivory-coated chairs that lined the walls.

The floors had been dusted with flavored sugar. Specks of it still sparkled in the corners, traces left when our hosts brushed it up before opening the doors to us. Burnt sugar, · vanilla cream — both scents hung in the air, and I tasted them when I licked my lips.

Leaning over Mattie's shoulder, I turned the card so I could consider the program. I could take refreshments during the lively numbers, for I had no intention of laughing and twirling with anyone through a schottische.

Touching the first waltz listed, I said, "Let's find Wills and Charlie."

Mattie narrowed her eyes and pulled the card from me. "We didn't come to dance with cousins."

"I think that's all I'm up to," I answered. I felt no need to embellish that; she saw my locket and knew me well enough. Digging in my heels didn't have to be a production for all to see.

"Once you get onto the floor, you'll enjoy it!"

I leaned my head against her shoulder. "I'm out of practice, Mattie."

"Let's get it over with, then." Distracted, she patted my

hand as she peered into the growing crowd. "The first is the worst, I imagine."

There were familiar faces here—our cousins, our school friends, some already turning on the floor in a quadrille. They shone with a glittered pleasure, all the whiteness of the room giving the impression that we were meant to be dancing at a wedding.

Perhaps we were.

Touched with melancholy, I started to tell Mattie that I would just watch, but she clutched my hand. It amazed me, how tight her grip could be when she wished it.

"Do you see that one there?" she asked, all breathless delight. "I think he's coming for us."

I turned toward her nod and chilled.

That he came for us was a certainty—or, at least, that he came for me. His overlong hair swept back in dark waves, Poe's Visitor from the burying grounds strode toward us. Befitting the surroundings, his coat was a better cut than the one I'd seen him in before—this one buttoned, dark velvet that suited his complexion.

But either he owned just one shirt or he badly used all that he owned. When he offered his hand to Mattie, I couldn't help notice that these cuffs as well were freckled with ink.

"I apologize for introducing myself," he said, taking

Mattie's hand with a slight nod before turning to me. "I didn't want to leave it to chance."

Disarmed before she could snap open her fan, Mattie used me to play shy. She turned toward me, casting a gaze at him over her shoulder. "You wicked, wicked creature."

"I may be wicked, but please, call me by my name," he said. Bowing to her, he elaborated, "Theo de la Croix."

"Matilda Corey," Mattie said, already giddy for him.

I prayed in that moment, prayed with fervor, that he would be enchanted by her. He should have been; Mattie was a confection. Clear skin, clear eyes, lovely mouth—she danced beautifully and flirted cleverly. *Please let her please him,* I begged.

But if she had, it didn't show.

"Zora Stewart." Pressing a flat smile to my lips out of courtesy, I offered my hand, though I didn't want to.

"A singular honor," Theo said. What a well-kept smile he had, measured in precise angles. His gaze lingered on me, but he turned his attention to Mattie. "May I write in your program, Miss Corey?"

Delight lifted Mattie's brows as she relinquished her dance card. Subtly, she shifted, brushing against his arm as she leaned to see where he'd scrawl his name. Sugared as the air, Mattie produced her fan and clutched it. "Oh, the polka. I do hope I can keep up."

He noted her charm long enough to be gracious, then turned dark eyes on me. "And your dance card, Miss Stewart?"

"I haven't got one," I said.

I tried not to be pleased with myself, truly I did. But when Mattie made a troubled sound, I had to fight back the urge to smile. To force me to dance, she'd have to relinquish *her* treat, and that—I knew quite plainly—would never happen.

Gently, I folded my hands together; gently, I smiled at Theo. Mattie clung to his arm like ivy. "Kindly excuse me. I could use some air."

And I did not turn back, ignoring two protests as easily as one. Instead, I glided through the crowd, through tall, arched doors to the brick portico in back. Lawns and rose gardens spread into the distance, and I gathered my shawl round my shoulders. I'd been warned all my life of the sicknesses carried by the night air, but I walked into the dark fearlessly.

Music played on behind me, richer as it stretched into the night. I followed the terrace down, winding through the spindly attentions of new rose vines.

Away from the ballroom, artifice and sugar faded and I found myself gazing into a pool of water stirred by an automatic fountain. It was a novelty to see water run without a pump or tap.

I tucked my gloves away. Gingerly, I reached out to feel the stream cascade over my palm. How pure and clean and cold it ran! I marveled at the sudden ache in my bones.

Get in, my thoughts urged—a perverse imp I hadn't heard in well over a year. I thought it had died entirely. And yet it sprang to life, daring me. I stole a look over my shoulder.

Pretty shadows danced through the windows, framed in marble. None, not one of those figures, turned to regard me. I could have been the last to walk the earth, down in this garden. Surrounded so, by a black band of sky and the strains of a distant violin, I thought that I truly might *be* the last.

Whim clicked in me, like the pin in a door finally catching. Raising my skirts, I stepped onto the fountain's wide, low wall and closed my eyes. The water sang now, breathing soft against my face.

A thousand icy pinpoints touched my cheeks, the well-deep chill streaming over me in waves. To the strains of a waltz, I walked the edge of the fountain. *No peeking,* my imp insisted. My chest felt full of bees, all buzzing wildly as I covered my eyes with my hand.

One step, and then a second. The little danger thrilled me and my senses turned keen. Intimately, I knew the water, the sureness of the stone—I wouldn't fall in, I couldn't—

I did, when Theo de la Croix called out to me.

Deceptively deep, the fountain swallowed me entirely. My beaded gown dragged me into the depths, and night, so appealing in the air, seemed a dark cap when filtered through icy water.

And yet, I felt peace. The cold, so sudden, the loss of breath, so complete—I struggled just once against it, then sank in grace.

Hard hands found me. They pulled me from the water that seemed not so much cold as tight around me. It was leaving it that racked me with a shuddering convulsion.

Laid on the lawn, rolled on my side, I felt very much a rag doll and coughed helplessly when the water drained from my nose and mouth.

"Miss Stewart!" Theo peered into my face. His breath felt of flame, touching my cheeks. "Are you hurt?"

I jerked when he clapped a hand against my cheek. I had frozen so completely that any touch came as pain. Struggling to sit, I shook my head and searched for my tongue, for anything at all to say.

But I suppose an unexpected dive into an unexpectedly deep fountain caused a commotion. How could it not, with the splashing and heroics. My end of the garden wasn't so distant from the party after all. Before I could find a thing to say, voices cried out and Theo and I turned toward them.

A clutch of dancers, fresh in their whites and their suits,

slowed to stop, their faces matching shades of shock. They stared, and shouldn't they stare, to see me lying beneath such a handsome boy, breathless and clinging?

A fresh lightness spilled through my veins when I realized my escape. "Not hurt, only ruined," I said.

"I haven't . . ."

"I'm sorry," I said, and pulled him into a kiss.

Stripped to my chemise, I perched by the stove. Clasping a cup of hot ginger tea and lemon, I warmed myself with sips of it. As pleasant heat filled me, it distracted me from the itch of the blanket draped over my shoulders.

Mama worried the floorboards bare as she paced the kitchen. "I expected Mattie to watch you a bit better than this."

"Mattie's not to blame," I said. I pulled my stool closer to the hot side of the stove, drinking up that warmth too. A disheveled mess, my hair clung to my face, some curls drying on my skin, most of the rest still heavy and damp from my swim.

A tempest, Mama whirled through the kitchen and stopped at the door to listen to my father. I had embarrassed him terribly, for one of his partners had been at the dance. Though Mr. Clare hadn't personally witnessed my disgrace, he *had* seen fit to bring me home.

"Out of deference to your father," Mr. Clare had told me sternly, urging the horses on. "For he's a good man who deserves better."

I'd considered leaping from his gig. I hadn't, because it would've been unfair to make him deliver to my parents news of my untimely demise rather than notice of my unseemly social death.

"In front of all Baltimore," Mama muttered, then spun round to face me again. "I've indulged you too often. Spoilt you. And what shall we do with you now?"

I should have been ashamed, but I smiled instead. "Lock me in the attic. I should say you could easily convince people of my insensibility."

Glowering, Mama plucked another stick up from the pile by the door and stuffed it in the stove. Though we had gas lighting through the rest of the house, Mama swore that nothing but wood and brick could cook a proper supper.

The bright scent of burning pine filled the kitchen, the only pleasure I had left when Mama plucked my cup from my hands. "Look at you, preening over this."

"Will Papa mind overmuch?" I asked disingenuously. I

couldn't imagine he would—matters of comportment and decency he generally left to my mother's discretion.

Mama finished my tea and put the cup aside. "I should think so, Zora Pauline. You've indebted him to Mr. Clare, embarrassed us all in front of him. That's our livelihood!"

A sliver of doubt lodged in my chest. Could it matter? Even Theo, poor, sad dupe that he was, would only be embellished by the incident. I was the one ruined; he'd earned a conquest.

But it pained me to think of Papa troubled by it, and I lowered my head. "If that's so, I'm sorry."

Mama snapped, "Good. I expect no less." Then, perhaps regretting her sharpness, she came to put her hands on my shoulders. "Oh, duck. I wish I knew what to do with you."

Sinking against her, I laid my cheek on her arm and murmured, "I did say it once—there's always the attic." When she pinched to punish my impertinence, I tipped my head to look at her. "I'll be quiet in daylight. Tell everyone you sent me west to stay with family."

My mother stilled, and I had learned that my mother's stillness could never bode well for anyone. Twisting on my perch, I looked at her quite directly. "Mama?"

I think she would have forgotten my suggestion entirely if a letter hadn't come for me the next day.

Postmarked Kansas, the envelope contained a note and a

photograph of a grizzled farmer and his weathered children. Lord above, I must have answered his advertisement for a bride—I hadn't considered how old a man with four sons might be.

Sheepishly, I hid my face while she read from his letter. In the middle, she stopped and fished out a paper cigar ring. Slapping it on the table before me, she informed me, "That's in lieu of a gold band, should his farm ever break even."

As a hot flush crawled my neck, I tried to find some valiant defense of myself. Instead, I only managed, "Well, he does need the help, doesn't he?"

"Enough," Mama said, collecting my mail-order proposal. "I'm wiring Birdie. She can put you to work, and maybe then you'll come to your senses."

What use my aunt might have for a slightly ruined, partly maddened eastern girl in Oklahoma Territory, I couldn't begin to imagine. But married or indentured, the result was the same.

I would be yoked, and I didn't mind at all.

Three

Through the gentle rise of the Allegheny Mountains, then on through woodland that turned to amber plains, I made my way by locomotive to Birdie's homestead in Oklahoma Territory. The train itself was pleasant enough most days, though the constant snow of coal ash through the windows made it impossible to keep anything clean—perhaps a portent of things to come.

From my window, I studied the villages blossoming along the rails, and considered my fate. I'd come to appreciate that Mama's way had advantages over mine. My methods— ruining myself, taking a husband—each required an infidelity I didn't wish to commit, not in truth. As my aunt's helper, I'd need never betray Thomas' memory.

Stepping from the train at Skeleton Ranch, I marveled at a sky that stretched boundlessly across the plains. The pure intensity of the blue stole my breath; at once, I was miniscule and infinite beneath it.

Then a sudden blast of heat snatched at my bonnet. I'd never felt such a wind, scorching and dry. In fact, I doubted entirely it was wind, because it seared and clawed, pulling my hair loose in spite of its pins. Baltimore's winds weren't always sweet, but they were always cool; they carried ever a taste of the ocean in them. They pushed, but never pulled.

Plucking a spray of tansy asters, I was glad to step into the black coach that would carry me to West Glory. Just a few more hours, and I'd be starting over. My new beginning had begun.

After four hours in the airless cab, however, I wasn't quite so optimistic. The schoolteacher who sat beside me chirped in terror each time we hit a bump in the road. And without any sort of pavement to follow, we hit quite a few.

But she wasn't as bad as the bachelors who sat on the seat across from us. Chaw stained their lips and their breath. What stank more than their gnawing mouths was the shared can into which they spat.

Though I had a bundle of bread and cheese for my lunch,

I couldn't bear to eat it, closed up as I was with chirping on one side and expectorating on the other.

The coach shuddered to a stop. My travel mates murmured among themselves, and I brushed the curtain back to peer outside. I saw no town on the horizon—only saddlebound men surrounding us. They pulled their reins hard, bits cutting into flesh. Their horses reared with agonized cries.

"Oh no," the schoolteacher whimpered.

She pulled a cross from her collar and started to pray. The coach jerked to one side, and she interrupted her devotions with a squeak. Sound swirled away for me; the dust outside fascinated my senses, leaving me numb to the realization that someone was crawling on the top of the coach.

The dust had a strange quality to it, like none I'd ever seen. Delicate stars flickered when sunlight streaked through it. Puffing and swirling, it danced in eddies and brooks around hooves in motion. And then, when someone threw our luggage from the stage, it rose in plumes, a great, waterless spring.

My trunk split when it hit the ground, revealing all I had in the world. Velvets and laces spilled out, trampled and kicked. Suddenly, I heard again; I saw more than the clouds of silken haze. I threw myself against the window.

My stamps! My writing papers! My dance card from the

Sons of Apollo Ball, half-filled, all crushed beneath iron shoes and wooden heels.

Furious, I reached for the door. What I thought to say, I can't imagine, and I had the latch all but open when one of the bachelors shoved me back into my seat.

"Just let 'em take it," he said.

Offended, I strained forward again. Who was he to handle me like that? No gentleman, that was certain. Sharply, I informed him, "That's all I have!"

The schoolteacher clutched my arm. "Don't give them cause to come in after us."

It occurred to me that she was afraid—that the bachelors were too. And I thought that perhaps I should have been. But what I felt was not the quavering chill of terror. It was indignation that my few mementos, trinkets worth nothing but sentiment, had been ground into the dirt.

"I'm sorry," I told them, and threw open the door.

❧

It was customary to help a lady from a coach. However, the shove from behind wasn't the usual method, nor was the slamming of the door. Nevertheless, I righted myself, lifting my chin when one of the highwaymen strode up to me.

"Lady, you better get back in there," he said.

A dirty rag covered most of his face, and a battered hat covered his head. There was nothing of him but a stripe of watery blue eyes beneath dark eyebrows. Long lashes caught the light, and his voice gave him away—younger rather than older, bravado instead of confidence.

"If you want my valuables," I told him, emboldened, "take them. But I'm collecting my dance card."

An unbearable hum started in my chest and rushed through me, fingertips to toes. Pushing past him, I hurried to my ruined trunk. Though my feet moved purposefully, I felt adrift—woozy on my own nerve. I snatched the dance card that still bore Thomas' handwriting, and my packet of stamps as well. I shoved both of them in my blouse for safekeeping.

A hand dropped on my shoulder, and I whipped around. Slipping my fan from my sleeve, I brandished it, as if I'd met this boy at a ball and not a robbery. "Mind yourself, sir."

Before he could answer, another bandit hopped down from the coach and started our way. His long brown coat flapped with each step, and he sounded like he might be amused. "Boy, what're you doing over there?"

"She won't get back in," the other said.

The answer came: "Make her!"

Petulant, he waved a hand at me. "What do you want me to do? Shoot her?"

In response, I heard the coach driver crack a whip. The stage groaned, then took off, speeding into the dust-laced distance. The older highwayman cursed, kicking at the luggage on the ground.

The high, dusty heat of the plains deserted me. Chilled into my bones, I found I couldn't quite take a breath. Until that moment, I had been submerged. Being abandoned pulled me to the surface—back into light and sound and realization. I stood in the middle of nowhere, beyond the bounds of etiquette, protected only by my wit and my ivory fan.

"You should be ashamed of yourselves," I said, manifesting a bit more of my madness. "Bad enough to make a career of thievery, but honestly. Look at the mess you've made."

The highwaymen exchanged glances. As I could see only their eyes, I couldn't tell what passed between them. But the older of the two grabbed my arm. Then he lifted, setting me off balance as he marched me to the side of the road like an unruly child.

"Sit down and shut up," he said, jerking me over ruts cut into the dirt.

The hum within me rose to a pulsing howl. My head

pounded with it; I felt it in my throat and my temple. I was alone—utterly alone in the wilderness, with two men of few scruples.

At once, lightning cracked so near, my ears rang and I tasted its acrid remains. The heavens opened with a deluge. Without my bonnet, which sat on the coach seat I'd abandoned, unexpected rain soaked my hair and ran down my face unimpeded.

Swallowing hard, I said, "I may shut up, but I will not sit on the ground in a corset and bustle."

"We need to go," his companion said, already saddled. Rain darkened his hat, and his horse twitched anxiously. "They're gonna beat us to town."

This bandit's eyes trailed my face, coming to rest just beneath my chin.

Instinctively, I reached for my locket. "It's tin. It's not worth anything."

"Then you won't miss it, will ya?"

His gloved hand covered mine, and he yanked. The ribbon snapped, and I felt it slip from my neck. Though his face was covered, I knew he was smiling. His eyes crinkled at the corners, a satisfied kind of smugness in the curve of his brow.

Then he mounted his horse and presented one more insult. He pulled the reins hard, turning the beast in deliberate circles on the remains of our luggage. New mud mixed by the rain coated everything with filth. It wasn't enough to rob me; he had to try to break me as well.

Finally, he rode off. In his wake, a piece of once-white lace fluttered weakly, a bird with a broken wing.

Though I suppose I could have, and might have been entitled, I didn't sit down and cry. Nor did I stand there waiting for rescue. I picked through the remains of my baggage, for cotton could be washed and lace could be mended.

Throwing a few sodden pieces over my arm, I turned to follow the coach's tracks. I'd survived much worse: my mother was right. I was alive—not the dreamy, rescued sort of survival I'd experienced at the fountain in Baltimore. This was a real and deliberate reclamation; I had rescued myself.

For the first time in a year, I felt alive, and I was glad of it.

When night came, cold came with it.

Putting my head down, I trudged on. Though the wagon path was clear enough—for it was the narrow stream of mud lined by prairie grasses on each side—I'd passed no sign for West Glory in my hours of walking. And I'd seen no evidence that these plains were inhabited by anything but an abundance of jackrabbits.

In a way, the cold relieved me. It distracted me from the growing fear that I might never make it to town at all. Surely if I'd walked that long in Maryland, I would have found *something*—a house, a traveler, the shore.

But Oklahoma Territory yielded nothing but a scrubby, never-ending plain. I wondered if the coach had arrived yet. If it hadn't, no one could know I'd gone missing. That meant no one would be looking for me.

Alone, I shivered.

The skies cleared, clouds parting like stage curtains to reveal a pure, black night. The stars went on and on, endless diamonds on the field above me. And though I saw my breath and felt my innards clench in hunger, I stopped to admire the constellations.

In that moment, I alone existed.

And then, with the rattle of wagon wheels, that moment ended.

Turning toward the sound, I squinted into the dark. A lantern danced in the distance, a firefly darting in the fields. It trundled toward me, and when I made out the shape of a wagon, I called out to it.

"You, there! Hello!"

I heard no answer, but the light shifted, turning toward me more directly. Giddiness bubbled in me, but I quashed it when I realized it could be the highwaymen come back to finish me. For a moment, I considered hiding.

But then I felt a tremor across my skin, as if I had rubbed some amber with silk. It raced through the earth beneath my feet, and though I couldn't place the source of it, it calmed me.

I waved my bit of lace again. "Hello! Over here!"

Finally, the wagon became more than a dark impression. It was a buckboard, not much more than four wheels and a spring-mounted seat, drawn by one chestnut horse. The driver stopped and lifted his lantern to better see me.

"What are you doing out here, miss?" he asked. His voice was warm as a summer afternoon.

Drawn to it, I wrapped my arms around my filthy bundle and came closer. "My coach was robbed on the way to West Glory. They left me here, and then it rained. I may be lost . . ."

He smiled faintly. "You *may* be lost."

"I might not be," I insisted. "I don't know for sure."

Tying the reins to the buckboard, he picked up something long from his seat and jumped down with the lantern. When he approached, I realized it was a rifle. The dark barrel gleamed in the moonlight, a long, certain threat that he carried comfortably.

Seeded with doubt, I stepped back. "Just tell me if I'm on the right path. I can keep walking."

"There are wolves out here," he said. He waved the gun and nodded at the expanse around us. "Bears and bobcats, too."

All the wildlife I'd experienced had been found at the circus with Papa. Though he preferred marveling at the tricks and stunts, he indulged me with a walk through the menagerie. That oiled tent had smelled feral, and the air dangerous, but those beasts were kept in cages. Most of them napped during my visit—the flies were more ferocious than the lions. I was big enough to admit I didn't care to meet any without steel between us.

I erased my step back and asked, "Is it far to town?"

"Yep." He bent his knees and held out a hand, waiting for me to take it.

It took me a moment to realize he meant for me to step on him—that he would be my block to climb into the buckboard. Though it made utilitarian sense, I blushed when I took his hand and raised my foot to do so.

"You're certain?" I asked.

He raised his face, my first real glimpse of him. He was

young, his skin unlined, though berry brown from the sun. Because of the low light, I couldn't be certain of his eyes, but they seemed very golden under his thick brows. Squinting at me, he gave another mysterious smile and said, "Very."

Stepping on him, as if I were Marie Antoinette of the Plains, I hurried to tuck in my skirts. The wet pile of my laundry made for a poor blanket, but I was too grateful to be off my feet to care.

"Name's Emerson Birch," he said, climbing in on the other side. The buckboard tilted with his weight, and I swayed toward him.

Our shoulders nearly brushed, but I righted myself straightaway. I could only imagine what my Aunt Birdie would think, to have me come into town with a young man and no chaperone. I didn't dare let it come across more unseemly than it was.

And when he propped the rifle between us, it was quite easy to maintain my side of the seat. The gun smelled of fresh black powder, and my throat tightened. I stared stalwartly forward, and I willed my thoughts toward any pleasant subject, to think on games of forfeit, or stars, or even a home-cooked meal.

But the rich, burnt scent of a gun recently fired demanded my attention—commanded my memory. I would, without my leave, see Thomas fall again and again, until I closed my eyes and forced out a reply.

My voice was thin as chalk, and I clutched the rail tightly. "Zora Stewart. A pleasure to make your acquaintance."

"I see you heard the rumors about my driving," he said. Unwinding the reins, he offered them to me. "I can point the way if you'd rather. Epona's easy enough." He nodded toward the horse, his gaze still on me.

Shaking my head, I pressed my hand to my chest. The dance card I'd stuffed into my blouse was stiff, and it comforted me. "You're kind to offer, but thank you, no."

He urged the horse forward, and soon we glided across the prairie, the buckboard a boat on a smooth lake. The ride jolted me too much to sleep, though I wished for it.

So, instead, I took in the strange new night all around me. The air smelt of fresh earth and green grasses—cleaner than the city, unencumbered by the closeness of neighbors upon neighbors.

The length of the day weighed me down. I wondered if my aunt would be angry or relieved to have me turn up in this condition. And, selfishly, I wondered if she might not have put back a bit of dinner, hoping to see me arrive. I caught myself so completely in these wonderings that I barely noticed when the wagon stopped.

When I looked up, I saw no town. Just a small cabin and, beside it, a lean-to big enough for one horse. Confused, I turned to Emerson and asked, "Where are we?"

"Home," he said. He tied the reins again and turned to me. "West Glory's another hour's drive. I'll take you in the morning."

"I can't possibly impose on your family," I said. Wound tight, I touched my bedraggled hair, my filthy collar. I did have a measure of pride, and it flared in horror at the thought of barging in unannounced, at my most unappealing.

Emerson handed me the lantern, and hopped from the bench. "You won't be. It's just me."

I stared. "I can't spend the night with you!"

"All right, then. Take that rifle there, orient yourself north, and start walking." He pulled a brace of rabbits from behind his seat. "It's twenty-five miles yet, I imagine."

Measuring his profile, I sat in dazed silence. He was alone in the Territories — but he couldn't have been any older than I was. It didn't make sense.

When he rounded the back of the wagon, I told him, "I don't handle arms."

"Is that so?"

"It is!"

Coming to my side, he peered up at me. His lips curled in

a maddening smile, and he said, not unkindly, "Go home, Zora Stewart. You're not gonna make it out here."

Then he tipped his hat to me, took his lantern, and went inside.

Four

I've always preferred my dramatics on the stage.

So I admit I rolled my eyes as I pushed my sodden dresses aside. Marie Antoinette no more, I hefted myself to the ground, clinging to the buckboard's iron rail until my feet touched the earth.

Though the prairie rose high and dark around me, I pushed down my nerves and put myself to unhitching Epona from the gig. She was sleek and smooth, casting off heat from her long drive.

Pulling straps to free her from the buckboard's shafts, I murmured apologetically when she bucked her muzzle against my hand. My pockets were decidedly empty of anything she might consider a treat.

As I freed her, a yellow slice of light fell on me. Glancing over my shoulder, I saw Emerson silhouetted in the door. Tall and lean, he seemed fixed in place — watching me, I supposed. Then he broke free and started in my direction.

"What do you think you're doing?"

Though I felt it quite obvious, I said, "You ran this poor creature for miles, then flounced off to make a statement. I'm minding her the way you should have."

Emerson took the reins. "I didn't flounce."

"Oh, you're quibbling." I stepped away and took my turn watching him. It was only fair, and I was rewarded.

Every motion he made was sure, rippling across his broad shoulders. His suspenders cut the strong line of his back in an X and pulled his breeches tight against his narrow hips.

My face went hot, and I turned away. Shame on me for considering any of it; shame on me twice for brazenly admiring a stranger, regardless of the dark. I retrieved my filthy laundry and retreated into the house, uninvited.

It was as small inside as it had seemed without. There were no rooms proper — there was simply *a* room. A potbelly stove sat against the back wall, marking the cabin in half.

To its right sat a table and a single chair, rough-hewn and golden — the dining room, kitchen, and parlor in one.

The brace of rabbits waited there for cleaning, illuminated by a tin lantern. Their glassy eyes shone in the light, unjudging.

I turned from them and found myself staring at Emerson's bedroom. He'd left his narrow rope bed unmade, straw jutting from the ticking at odd angles. The quilt was worn, its flags of brown and green calico faded.

Heat stroked the back of my neck. Standing alone in a young man's boudoir could lead to ruin, but then, wasn't I already ruined? My heart fluttered in my chest and set to aching when I wondered what Thomas would think of all this.

The door opened, and I smoothed myself over. Clasping my hands together, I offered Emerson a whitewashed smile. "You built all this yourself?"

"I did." He barred the door, then hung his rifle on hooks above it. A bag swung from his other hand, and as he moved through the small space, the air stirred. The rough, sweated scent of his skin filled the cabin, mingling with gunpowder and leather.

Turning eyes to me, he asked, "Are you hungry?"

A strange trembling moved through me. Folding my skirts, I pressed my back against the wall. "Yes. My lunch pail left with the coach."

He spilled the contents of the sack onto the table—a

handful of scrubby onions and potatoes. Without thought, I picked up the rabbits and took his hunting knife in hand.

I leaned down, taking account of the tin buckets beneath his table. One was stained black around the rim, and I chose that one to put between my feet to clean the rabbits. His was a good knife, and I heard Mama in my head rhapsodizing about the right tool for the right job.

"What do you think you're doing?"

Glancing up from my work, I said, "It's not my kitchen. I haven't the first idea where your well is. Or if you've got any grease or flour, or whether you've got pots set back. I'm afraid you'll have to do the cooking, Mr. Birch."

"It's just Emerson," he said.

He stood there a moment, then shook his head at me. As if I were some confounding creature, and perhaps I was. Nevertheless, he made himself busy as well. Soon enough, we had a pot of rabbit stew bubbling away.

Emerson led me outside so we could wash our hands. The well was a simple affair, a wooden lid covering a hole he'd dug in the ground. He lowered the bucket down, bringing up barely a cup of clear water. Frowning, he offered it to me first. "It was fine in the spring."

"It's in the wrong place," I told him.

I don't know why I said it; what did I know of wells? But

the meager water I poured over my hands smelled of rain, not the earth. There was a greenness to it, distance in it — cool only because it had collected in the shade, not because it had sprung up from the depths.

"Then where would you suggest, Miss Stewart?" he asked. It was clear he didn't expect an answer. In fact, he came across quite snide, and some old measure of pride leapt up in me.

Lifting my chin, I said, "Give me a moment."

The prairie spread out wide around me, and I drew my gaze across it slowly. Something had planed this land flat — it was smooth as a looking glass, except for a few dark trees so far in the distance I could hardly tell if they were saplings or grown.

But I walked toward them in the star-speckled dark; with the cabin behind me and the horse's soft whickers nearby, I felt quite safe. My heart insisted it could find water, though my mind disagreed. I would make a fool of myself for bragging, I thought — but my heart beat and a strange coolness came over me.

I closed my eyes and breathed in deep — until I smelled water, fresh and clear. I felt it pulsing like a heartbeat, drawing me toward it. My bones ached, as if I'd jumped into a winter sea. It was very like the peace I'd felt when my skirts dragged me into the fountain — I wasn't frightened at all; it was an embrace.

When I opened my eyes, a faint glimmer snaked across the plains. Silvery, ghostly streams marked the land, as if the water that moved beneath the earth had revealed itself to me.

My deep breath sustained me through the shock. Presented with a wonder, with a marvel, I disbelieved it at first. But the light did not fade at my doubt — no, it seemed to call me. It sang, not with music but with sensation, a siren that lured me into motion.

Unsteady, I stumbled toward the brightest, nearest spot. When I came to stand on top of it, a bright intoxication filled me. It was magic — real magic, and though I'd seen my cousin Amelia give a hundred fortunes, though I had seen so many of them come to pass — some part of me had yet resisted belief. There was still a rational thread in me that said no magic could be true.

But in that moment, it broke.

Turning slowly over the silver of my vision, I knelt down to flatten my palm against the ground. My heart beat in time with the rhythm beneath me. The earth was alive, running with pure, clear water — I had no doubt of it whatsoever.

I struggled to find my voice, and when I did, it came out as a spare whisper. "Right here. Dig your well here."

Speaking broke the moment. All the glimmering rivers drained into the dark. I made a soft sound of disappointment. How strange it was to be newly habituated to a marvel, so much that I missed it as soon as it was gone. I saw only night and felt a bit foolish.

But when I raised my head, Emerson Birch stood over me. His smirk had faded. Offering me his hand, he said, "First thing tomorrow."

"See you do," I blustered, standing without his help.

Realizing the cool of the night, I bundled myself in my arms again, starting inside. Papa used to joke that we came from a long line of charlatans and dowsers, and that's why taking up the law was so natural to him. Now it seemed I carried on the family legacy, entirely by accident.

Emerson and I shared dinner in quiet. He didn't try to make conversation, and I, in my newly magicked state, couldn't find words that mattered enough to voice.

Truly, I'd spent a summer extolling Amelia's miraculous sunset visions—I had pushed her and praised her—and now, it seemed, I emulated her. It was an impossible thing suddenly possible, and my heart thrummed in odd rhythms.

How peculiar that I should oppose her element, that she

would be fire and now I imagined myself water. I could only take it to mean that the madness of my grief lingered, just in another shape.

"Take my bed," Emerson said.

His voice interrupted my thoughts but not my daze. I should have argued. I should have been the one to wrap myself in a quilt by the stove and sleep on the floor.

But I wasn't, and I was punished for it with a long night of distraction. The linens smelled of him, and I felt the pulse of water outside. When I sank down to dreams, they were troubled and odd.

This was not the first day in the West I had expected, and I had a most unsettling sense that none of the others would be either.

~~~~~~

West Glory jutted up from the prairie like a single ship in a sea of grass. As Emerson steered the buckboard closer to the one street that ran through it, I found myself disappointed.

Frontier stories were among my favorites; when I was small, Papa would read Buffalo Bill's dispatches from the Territories at bedtime, instead of fairy tales or parables.

So in all my planning to come to the rugged West, I'd expected to see long-coated gunslingers swaggering along. Certainly, there should have been ladies of questionable repute wearing nothing but petticoats and corsets as they called to passersby. Dirty miners, cowboys running cattle through the street, and Indians in buckskins watching it all suspiciously from a distance — I truly believed I should see them all there.

I had built the West into a foreign world in my mind, and it was. Simply not the one I'd imagined.

West Glory boasted a whitewashed church and wooden sidewalks — those, at least, came as I expected. But the false fronts of the stores were painted in gay colors, bright sparks among the gold of the prairie and the gray of the dust.

Though it seemed most of the women wore loose corsets or none at all, their blouses and full skirts were entirely familiar to me — exactly what my mother wore to work in the kitchen; what I would have worn if I had gone to clerk in my father's office.

An Indian woman crossed in front of us. Her black hair flowed loose down her back, and her clothes — though different from mine — were made out of familiar cotton and calico. She wore no paint or feathers, and I had begun to suspect that Buffalo Bill's dispatches from the West were, at best, embellishments and, more likely, fictions.

The starkest difference was that all the men seemed to go in dungarees and shirtsleeves, held together by suspenders. Without jackets and ties, and often without hats, they were shockingly *visible*.

Whenever my gaze trailed to Emerson, I had to snatch it away again. I had no business noticing his muscles, well developed from working the land, through his blue cambric shirt. And, I reminded myself, I did Thomas' memory a terrible disservice for wanting to look at all.

"Where does your aunt live?" Emerson asked.

His voice startled me, so I reached for my suitcase. It took a moment to remember it was gone. All I had left was a bundle of filthy dresses, some ruined stamps, and a dance card.

Folding my hands in my lap, I kept my eyes forward and said, "I'm not entirely sure. We've always sent letters to Birdie Neal, West Glory, and they arrived."

"We'll stop at the post office, then."

The sweet scent of apple pie suddenly caught my attention. I turned to find its source—the little restaurant beside the general store was my best guess. It would have been decadent to have pie for breakfast, but I was starving. Emerson and I had shared the remains of the rabbit stew between us—a modest meal compared with the one I would have had at home.

No, I told myself. *This is home now.*

The moment Emerson stopped the buckboard, I let myself down. He protested handsomely, and I thought it just a little funny to leave him cursing under his breath in my wake.

But my smile faltered when I stepped inside and saw the clerk behind iron bars. For a moment, I wondered if I hadn't walked into the jail by mistake—Emerson would be the one laughing then, wouldn't he?

But the clerk cleared his throat at me. "Got something to post, miss?"

Stirring through the still heat, I approached the counter. "No, sir. But could you tell me where I can find Mrs. Beatrice Neal? I know that she has several acres nearby, but I'm not entirely sure where."

The clerk disappeared beneath the counter, then rose again with a groan. Flopping a giant ledger open, he flicked through pages efficiently, then turned it toward me. "This here is the town district. You want to head three miles northeast, more or less. If she's got her lot stake still up, it'll be 325."

"Three miles northeast, plot 325," I repeated.

He let me look at the book a moment more, then snapped it closed. "Anything else I can do you for?"

"No, no, thank you," I said, turning for the door. Then I

turned back, my curiosity too sharp to ignore. "Actually, pardon me for asking, but why have they got you caged up like that?"

The clerk narrowed his eyes at me, then smiled. Running a hand through his salt-and-pepper hair, he said, "Because I'm just that damned irresistible, darling."

My face flushed, and I hurried outside. Emerson loitered at my side of the buckboard. When he caught sight of me, he frowned. "What's the matter?"

The attention only deepened my blush. Squeezing Emerson's hand overhard, I all but leapt into the wagon. "Three miles northeast, plot three two five."

My voice came out brittle, which made me seem more unsettled than I was. Honestly, I'd been flirted with before—I'd been in love, I'd been kissed. And, I reminded myself wryly, I had kissed a total stranger in front of all Baltimore. But no one had ever spoken to me with that kind of—I didn't even know what to name it! Lust? Deliberation?

When Emerson climbed up beside me, I turned on him and demanded, "Why is the clerk in a cage, in truth?"

"To keep people from stealing the mail." He stared, as if thinking better of asking, but ask he did. "Why?"

"Sheer curiosity."

Emerson laughed, bafflement clear in the slope of his

brows. But he said nothing else; he simply urged Epona in the right direction. Just as quickly as we'd come to West Glory, we'd exited, and I was glad to leave it behind.

A strange, earthen lump greeted us three miles northeast.

"What is that?" I asked, tipping my head slightly at what seemed to be a heap of mud and straw in the middle of the lot.

"Home, I reckon." When I stared at him, he clarified. "It's a soddy."

A soddy — a sod house. It looked dark and dank, as if the floor of a stable had risen up and cobbled itself into the vague shape of a building. My stomach clenched.

Compared with the soaring three stories of the row house at home, this soddy was terrifying. But I wouldn't be missish about it.

White chickens ran around it, chased by a little girl in a green pinafore. I guessed that must be my baby cousin Louella. Before I could call to her, she fled into grasses so high I couldn't make out the shape of her bonnet.

While I considered my new home, Emerson hopped down, his stride swift as he rounded the back of the wagon.

Since he seemed so completely determined to be a gentle-man today, I felt it my God-given duty to thwart him.

Despite his speed, I managed to let myself down before he arrived, and I fixed him with a sweet smile. He stood too close, and I tipped my head all the way back to look up at him.

Innocently, I said, "You're out of breath, Mr. Birch."

Reaching past me, he gathered my things and cut me a sharp look. "Pleased with yourself?"

"I am. Thank you for asking," I replied, then jumped when a woman's voice cut between us.

"Get your hands off my niece."

The crack of a shotgun being racked punctuated the order, and Emerson all but leapt away from me. Two things struck me when I turned toward my Aunt Birdie. The first, uneasiness that she raised a gun so quickly, the second, that she too was hardly older than I.

Though I knew Mama was Birdie's elder by fifteen years, I supposed I'd never considered what that meant. The tin-type of her in our parlor was young and fresh-faced. Her pale hair coiled like a crown on her head, and the clarity of her eyes was apparent, even without color to define them.

She was still that girl exactly—aside from the calico re-placing her serge, and the shotgun in her hands in place of a fan. I put my hands out and approached her, praying there'd be no scent of black powder when I came close. "He did me a kindness, Aunt Birdie. The stage was robbed, and he . . ."

Looking past me, Birdie gestured for Emerson to get back in his wagon. "Go on. I don't need you sniffing around here."

"He's not, he's—"

"Going, ma'am. Good luck to you, Miss Stewart." Emerson tipped his weatherbeaten hat at the two of us, then climbed back into the wagon. His voice was flat as slate, and he didn't meet my eyes. Bitter animosity weighed the air.

Birdie's brow smoothed, but she didn't lower the gun.

"Wait," I said. The wind kicked up, a hot breath that stirred the earth around us. A haze rose with it as I hurtled toward the buckboard. "Wait! My things!"

Reining Epona, Emerson dropped the sorry bundle of my laundry into my arms, then drove away in an ashen gout of dust. Whatever had passed between him and Birdie did more than baffle me; it angered me.

I could concede that Emerson did have a touch of arrogance to him, but he had, in fact, rescued me on the road. Given me a place to sleep for the night, protected me from the wolves. And then carried me into town and beyond it, just to see that I was safely delivered to my destination.

Pulling my shoulders back, I marched toward my aunt. Carefully, I measured my voice, asking instead of demanding, "Why would you drive him off like that, without even a cup of tea? He did nothing but see me to your door."

Birdie cracked the shotgun open again, dumping the shells in her hand. "It's for your own good, Zora. Nobody here knows what happened in Baltimore, and we'll keep it that way. But you can't go running around with Birch."

A protest flew to my lips—I had hardly intended to *go running around* with anyone, but to be forbidden without explanation? "Why can't I?"

"He stole that land he's living on," Birdie told me, clear green eyes narrowing. The expression marred her dollish features. "He's as bad as those Dalton Gang boys, and I don't want him around."

My skin tingled—not quite numbness, almost a sort of fire. Emerson hardly struck me as a thief or a murderer, and certainly as nothing less than a gentleman, however rough his manner. And I raged inwardly that a single, calculated kiss had so lowered my aunt's opinion of me, sight unseen.

"But he—"

Already frustrated, Birdie dropped the shotgun shells into her apron pocket and directed me toward the soddy. "It's for your own good." Then, as if realizing we were strangers and hardly introduced, she turned to catch my face between her hands. The hardness in her eyes faded. "You look just like your mother."

"Do I?" I asked automatically.

Stroking a rough thumb against my cheek, Birdie seemed caught in memories for a moment—pleasant ones, at least, for the corner of her mouth turned up in a wry smile. "Very much so. Come inside. We'll have some tea before we start the laundry."

She nudged me toward the door, then raised her voice to call, "Louella! Louella Lou, come home! Come meet your cousin Zora!"

Ducking inside the soddy, I tried not to be surprised. Earth floor and earthen walls made for a cool but dark little house. What should have been windows were holes with oilpaper tacked over them. They let in just enough light for me to realize that my aunt had a very spare life indeed.

I put myself to work building a fire in the squat iron stove. She had hard, golden sticks in the wood box. Examining them closely, I realized they were bundles of straw, braided and folded.

In Baltimore, we would have boiled the water for the washing in the kitchen, but there was hardly room for that in the soddy. I decided there must be a fire pit outside somewhere, which meant stoking that as well.

This simple plan thrummed through me, and I was unnerved that the prospect of chores gave me pleasure. But something hard, to work the muscles and settle the mind, sounded delicious.

It would scrub away my leftover, unseemly thoughts about Emerson—whose company I shouldn't have been so distressed to be denied. I stood on this land, in this country, to be my aunt's helpmeet and to do honor to the life I would have had, if Thomas were still at my side.

A wistful pang went through me. I wondered what Thomas would have thought about a soddy. If he would have greeted this as an adventure or a hardship. But then, we'd planned to settle in Annapolis, hadn't we? A city well established—plenty of brick and wood to make a strong house there.

Brushing those thoughts away, I focused on the fire. The straw logs burned much the way wood did. I watched them all the same, for the novelty of it, I suppose. Settling into this place, thick walled and cool except by the stove, I marveled that I could hear little from the outside.

I felt just as safe in these walls as I had within the more familiar sort of Emerson's cabin. And when I took a deep breath, I smelled spring water all around, running pure beneath the parched earth. I had a feeling that my aunt's well was dug deep and true, and that comforted me.

There was no good reckoning why I had abided by the water in Baltimore, living on the shore and tasting it in the wind, but it was here in these dusty plains that I called it to me. But I did, and knowing I could look into the dark and see water flowing silver in the distance gave me peace.

It was something wholly new; it made me new — I was Zora Stewart, but no longer the same.

Five

But just as a strong pulse is needed to move a body, it needs breath as well. And when Birdie introduced me to the yoke I'd need to haul water, I wasn't sure I'd ever get a full breath again.

"It's only heavy at first," she told me.

Indeed, though it looked like a wooden railroad tie, she hefted it with ease. Someone had smoothed a curve into the center of it, which I discovered was the place it was meant to sit on my shoulders. A small notch accommodated the back of my neck. Thankfully, it was sanded smooth.

But it didn't fit well. Nor was it light. Though it was vaguely balanced, I still felt like a clumsy scarecrow when Birdie hung pails on either end.

Wobbling, I swayed first to one side, then so violently to the other that I dropped the first bucket. Then the other bucket slid the length and cracked against my bare hand.

"Maybe you should walk up and down a ways first," Birdie said, reclaiming the pails. They were wooden, with rusted bands holding them together. My suspicion was that she was primarily concerned about *their* well-being, not mine.

Rebalancing myself, I took a few tentative steps. The thing was awful—hot and heavy—but I was determined to master it. Sweat kissed the nape of my neck, and my chest burned. I wanted to draw in deep, but whalebone and silk restrained me.

Nonetheless, I circumnavigated the soddy twice and was almost proud of myself. At least, until my dear cousin, the chicken tormenter, shrieked through and sent me tumbling.

"Louella, enough!" Birdie had not one hint of amusement or indulgence in her voice.

I lay in the dirt, staring into a sky bright enough to sting my eyes. Blinking through my blindness, I pressed my elbows into the ground. That stirred the fine dust, which turned my nose to twitching. Now I had stunted two senses as I sprawled there.

My corset's steel conspired against me; for all my might, I couldn't push myself up. Flopping against the hard pillow of the yoke, I gazed helplessly at the sky once more. Still boundless, its expanse mocked me, stretching everywhere when I could do nothing but lie there.

Then Louella's face filled my sight as she came over to poke at me. "Mama says I'm sorry."

"I am too," I replied. I held my hand out to her, "Can you help me up?"

With puppyish grunts, Louella pulled as hard as she could. And for a moment, I thought I might be freed, but she lost her grip. She sat down hard, and I thumped my head on the yoke when I slipped back again.

"For Pete's sake," Birdie said. She didn't finish the thought, but in a blur of motion, she lifted Louella out of the dirt, then hauled me to my feet as if I were made of nothing more than down.

Looking me over, she sucked a breath through her teeth. Her eyes narrowed, seeing straight past my gown and into my undergarments. It was plain she measured my corset with her gaze; then, without mercy, she said, "Go take it off."

"Let me take out the busk stiffener," I bargained.

Birdie didn't indulge *me*, either. "You can keep it for Sundays and callings, but I've got no use for you if you can't bend down or stand up on your own."

My face flamed. Oklahoma Territory had no end of indignities, it seemed. A welcome by robbery and gunpoint, a first night in a stranger's bed, and now the loss of my corset. I didn't want to be precious, truly I didn't, and I *could* see Birdie's point.

But I still stung as I hunched beneath the raw ceiling of the soddy. It struck me then, as I worked a myriad of buttons and peeled off layer after layer, that whether I wanted to be precious or not, I certainly was. Standing there in my chemise and drawers, I folded my corset and put it in a shelf dug out of the wall.

Prickles crawled my skin, and I realized that this little house had its advantages. It was cooler than the open fields, for certain. Once I could breathe deep, I smelled the freshness of it, the rich, welcoming cool of a root cellar, only above ground.

Pulling my petticoats and dress back on, I searched my own body with my hands. I felt rather like jelly poured out of its glass. I held my shape but wobbled all the same.

"Let me try again," I told Birdie when I stepped outside once more.

It was strange—I felt the sun more directly through my gown, and the wind more directly as well. The yoke, though heavy yet, settled more comfortably on my shoulders, now that it wasn't compressing me into my stays.

"Lou can show you the well," Birdie said, hanging the

pails on the yoke again. "Just fill them halfway at first, until you get used to it. Do your best to get that basin filled; I need to work on some lace for Caroline in town."

"Yes, ma'am," I said, then squared myself to do as she asked. I had taken only a few steps into the prairie when I heard her call after me. Turning toward her, I managed to stay on my feet—quite an accomplishment in itself. "Yes?"

Birdie put her hands on her hips and told me with a scrap of sympathy in her voice, "You'll get used to it."

And I doubted not at all when I replied, "I'm sure I will."

~~~~~~~~

Standing over the little stove, Birdie swirled her wooden spoon in a bubbling pot. Her glances in my direction became rare as I proved I was perfectly capable of holding Louella in my lap and showing her how to stitch on her little piece of muslin.

"Do you want to see my favorite?" I asked.

Glad to be done, Louella became an anchor in my lap and laid her head against my shoulder. I turned the fabric around, trying to smooth a spot. The scrap had seen far better days, though. Once, it was cream colored; now it was dark as a shadow on its edges, and varying shades of gray throughout.

"All right, duck," I said. Finding my fingers, I started a border on the scrap. A little, ornate chain appeared with my careful sewing. "This is a chained featherstitch. Do you see how it loops and joins up?"

Louella nodded, and Birdie looked back at me. "Don't do anything you can't pick out. Thread's dear." Then, as she turned back to her pot, I heard her mutter, "But then, what isn't?"

Quiet, I told Louella, "I have a world of experience picking stitches back out. But let's put some in. Look, I'm going to make a pretty pattern with it."

Stuffing a finger in her mouth, Louella swayed, watching my stitches bloom on her cloth. Her lashes kept falling, and I thought very much that she might sleep right there on my lap.

It was sweet for me, how warm and real she was in the curve of my arms. How useful I felt, though I was hardly teaching her anything at this point. Her hair smelled of sunshine and prairie grass, burned clean by the land.

Tempered by her calm, I found myself drifting pleasantly too. My fingers danced, and the needle slipped between them like a silver fish leaping over waves. The muslin shimmered, the same way the prairie did when the wind rushed across it.

On the horizon of the edge, past the stitched field of grain I made, it seemed very dark. Without thinking, I murmured to Birdie as I turned the scrap again. "Will the chickens go in their coop if it storms?"

"If such a thing ever happened, they would," she replied.

"It rained on me yesterday, and I think it's going to again."

"From your lips to God's ears. We didn't get a drop, and we could use it," Birdie said. "I'll be lucky if my corn row is ankle high by July."

I hummed softly, my embroidered field growing. It flourished with each sway, and each fluttering sigh from the baby in my arms. Rubbing my face against Louella's silky cheek, I repeated, "I do think it will."

A crack of thunder agreed.

Though the thick sod walls insulated us from the sound, it startled Louella from her near-nap. She slid from my lap and threw open the front door. What we hadn't seen through the oilpaper windows was the sky kneading itself darker and darker. Faint, lavender veins of heat lightning coursed through the clouds.

Any sky could threaten, and lightning meant nothing when it was the threadlike, embroidered sort. But the wind

turned, and it smelled of rain—that distant, heavy greenness that comes before a storm.

Leaving my sewing on the little chair, I said, "I'm going
to put the chickens in, just in case."

"You do that," Birdie said, and I felt her eyes on me all
the way out the door.

~~~~~~

Chickens, it turned out, rather liked the rain.

I'd had a devil of a time getting them into the coop the
night before, and the following morning they splashed in the
mud like unruly children.

"They're eating bugs," Louella said, standing over the
chickens instead of scaring them out of their wits.

And she wasn't wrong—the storm had scoured the night,
leaving morning full of twisting worms and newly bloomed
flowers.

Even the sky seemed scrubbed clean. The horizon that
just yesterday faded into a dusty haze now stretched on forever. When I squinted, I made out the shape of another
homestead in the distance.

It gleamed gold in the early light, a timber house instead
of a soddy. A curl of smoke rose from it, another family in
the wilderness breaking their fast. Something about that

made my heart swell. The world went on around me, and we were all connected by earth and rain and the bobbing heads of poppy mallow and indigo.

This is a good place.

I didn't so much think it as feel it—a certainty that didn't settle in the marrow of my bones but emerged from it. I smiled at the basin we'd set out, now full of rainwater to wash our clothes. Though my breast and bone still protested the lack of a corset, I had to admit I found the way the wind slipped through my clothes a singular pleasure.

"Time for breakfast," I told Louella.

I would have picked her up, but she'd run outside without stockings or shoes, and now she, like the chickens, wore a layer of mud. I laughed when she ran straight inside—yet another advantage to a soddy. Louella could hardly track mud in on a dirt floor!

"I'll be heading into town this week," Birdie said as she sat with a tin pan in her lap. She'd baked a bit of corn cake and boiled last night's beans again to heat them. Louella got the biggest share of both because she was growing, but even her portion was small.

As Birdie offered neither honey nor butter, I didn't ask for them. But, shamefully, I missed them desperately. The beans tasted only of beans and a bit of salt; the corn cake was gritty—not sweet or light the way Mama's cornbread was. My mouth watered for breakfasts I had bolted down without thought in Baltimore: fresh eggs, and bacon, and hotcakes shining with maple syrup.

Apparently, my memories played on my face, for Birdie put her fork down and said, "I know this isn't much, but Caroline will be paying me for this month's lace soon. We'll have a proper dinner to welcome you then."

Embarrassment slapped my cheeks scarlet. "This is good."

"No, it's not." Birdie snorted and picked her fork up again. There was no sadness in it, simply matter-of-factness. "I've been putting a dollar aside each month to get a hog or a cow."

"Milk," Louella sang, chasing a bean around her plate.

"Yes, probably a calf," Birdie agreed. "It's a hard thing to balance. With a cow, we'd have milk and butter and cream, and it'll happily feed itself through the summer."

Though I had never considered what keeping animals might mean, I guessed the converse. "Whereas a pig won't do anything but demand feed and scraps for months, until it's big enough to slaughter?"

Impressed, Birdie nodded. "Exactly right."

"I could take on some sewing too. My stitches are good, and . . ."

"No, ma'am." Birdie ladled a bit of the bean broth into

Louella's plate. "I need you to mind Louella and the chores. I can accomplish plenty of sewing when I'm not doing everything else. And if you keep Lou entertained, we might yet have some eggs."

My traitor stomach growled, and at that, my hard, hardworking Aunt Birdie threw her head back and laughed.

~~~~~

Thus, my first days on the prairie passed in hard labor.

The little vegetable patch behind the soddy drank all we could give it and then demanded more. So did Louella.

Water for farming, for drinking, for washing—all of it had to be carted by hand. It was the first task of each day, before I could start anything else.

Yesterday morning, I'd hauled water and grubbed for early wild onions and Jerusalem artichokes. Then came the afternoon. I hauled water and scrubbed Louella clean once the mud had dried up. After that, I hauled water for our dinner of thin pea soup and chicory tea.

Now, standing alone by the well, I glared at the yoke and gave it a little kick. No one was there to see me do it, and I thought I had earned a tantrum.

But I was annoyed by my own petulance. This was just what I had waited for, what I had begged for—a new life of labor in the West. And it wasn't awful—just hard, and tedious.

I bent to lay the yoke across my shoulders. Full buckets dangled on either end of it, held safe by grooves carved into the wood. Carefully, I rose to standing. I had gotten brave lately, carrying back full buckets. But that meant every step had to be deliberate lest I slosh all the water out between the well and the soddy.

I could hear my mother laughing from a distance, pointing out what a good lesson in posture this chore was. Though I imagined her amused, I certainly wasn't. I felt every inch bruised and battered and badly used.

It did little to soothe me to know I had yet to gather the laundry I'd left on top of swaying prairie grasses to dry. Marching back, I made pictures out of the clouds and hummed to myself.

A waltz measured my steps and reminded me fondly of Thomas. There were no tears in thinking about him at our first dance, asking for all my waltzes. Once I had danced in Irish lace, in my beloved's arms, to the intimate third-beat of Mr. Chopin's compositions.

My memories shortened the walk and drifted away like so much morning fog when I reached the yard once more. They left nothing but a sweet impression in my mouth, like the lingering flavor of a penny candy.

I poured my bounty into the basin Birdie had left in the yard. In a bit, I'd split it into dinner water and washing water. I took a moment to catch my breath.

Still, when Louella shrieked by, I plucked her off her feet. It was a kindness to the chickens, run ragged by her chasing, and a treat for me. She was a warm, squirming bundle, sweetened by wind and exertion.

"You're mine, mine, mine," I told her, rocking her like a baby in my arms.

Kicking her feet, Louella shrieked her reply. "No, no, no!"

My back protested, but I swung her around. Then it was my turn to shriek, because she flung herself headlong from my arms. Though I lunged to catch her, she was back on her feet and fleeing into the prairie again.

Lifting my skirts, I chased her, for the sun had dipped at the horizon, and Emerson's warnings against wolves and bobcats floated to the top of my thoughts.

Louella was nothing more than a shaking of the grass. I heard her laughter and saw the ripples she left in the field — the only traces I had to find her. Though she was small, she was sure-footed. *Perhaps half goat,* I thought uncharitably as I stumbled across the uneven ground.

Sweat soaked me beneath my dress; the prairie was deceptive in its openness, hiding vicious heat in the clarity of the air. By the time I caught a glimpse of Louella, I was dizzy and thought myself quite liable to swoon before I caught her.

But she stopped, then somehow rose above the tall green and golden grasses that swayed from here to the horizon. In my lightheadedness, I believed for a moment that she might jump up and take flight like a little mockingbird.

After all, hadn't I known a girl who could see the future? Had I not myself looked into the dark to see the veins of water flowing through the land? Why not a babe with the gift of wingless flight—would that be entirely impossible?

Stumbling into a clearing, I realized that my silly head *had* been dreaming the impossible. Louella had not floated, she'd jumped up—onto a rail of graying wood.

"That was a good chase," I said, swiping my brow with my sleeve. I approached, slowly so she wouldn't be tempted to run again.

"I won."

With a laugh, I murmured my agreement. And as I came closer I realized she balanced not on a rail but on a foundation of sorts. Wood had been joined together, stretching across the dry ground in a long rectangle. It didn't quite meet in the middle, and I realized as I walked through that space that someone had left room for a door.

Turning inside the border, I asked, "What is this?"

Louella held her arms out wide, walking the rail fearlessly. "Our house. Papa started it."

Inside my chest, my heart tightened. Birdie and her husband Petty had settled first in Kansas—that's where Louella was born. But when news of the land rush in the Territories came this year past, they moved to claim their 160 acres. It was free land to anyone willing to race for it. To care for it.

Walking the borders of the foundation, I tried to imagine what this would have been, if scarlet fever hadn't taken Petty.

I had only Emerson's cabin as a measure, but it was a good measure, I thought. This house would have been twice as wide. Room enough for a bedroom, for an iron stove; space enough for a family to spread out a bit come winter.

Nothing like the earthen cellar of the soddy, where Birdie had to take up the pallets each morning so there would be room to cook and eat and sew during the heat of day.

Standing in the middle of an unfinished promise, I rubbed the place where my locket had been. My fond remembrance at the well peeled away. In my own grief, the world had stopped. Having it start again so abruptly, on such a sharp reminder that my pain was hardly singular, I dammed my tears.

When Louella strayed near, I caught her hand. "It's getting dark, duck. Your mama will be wondering about us."

"I'm tired, Zora," she chirped.

Weary, I groaned. But when she put her finger in her mouth and implored me with big green eyes, I relented. Giving her my back, I said, "Hop on, then. No pulling my hair for reins."

And hop she did, nearly knocking me to my knees. Worse yet, she was hot. It felt as though I carried a burning coal on my back, one with wriggly little fingers that pulled my hair in spite of my admonition. Which turned out to be quite a bit better than when she felt her balance shift and threw both arms around my neck.

Half-strangled, I wheezed. The sounds I made sent Louella into peals of laughter, which—once I had extricated myself enough to breathe—made me laugh as well. We were a disheveled, giggling mess as we came around the soddy.

And so it was, with delight on my lips and a babe in my arms, entirely careless and hair pulled loose, that I met Mr. Theo de la Croix again.

Six

"Let go now," I told Louella.

I dipped low so she could slide off, then straightened. My hands flew immediately to my hair. There was no salvaging the chignon, so I did my best to smooth everything around it.

It wasn't that I wanted to pretty myself for him, though it was generally embarrassing to get caught out so discomposed. But what it did, however, was let me stall polite conversation so I could try to regain my composure.

Unfortunately, I failed and blurted out, "What are you doing here?"

"Where are your manners, Zora?"

Birdie's voice sounded tight, and when I caught a glimpse of her face, I noted the tension between her brows. Reaching out to take her hand, I forced the best smile I could and looked up at Theo again. "I mean, imagine my surprise. This is the last place I expected to meet you."

"Forgive me for that. It seems I'm always turning up unexpectedly on you," he said. His voice was creamy as I remembered it, warm like his skin and dark eyes. Perhaps in deference to travel, he'd pulled his glossy hair back and fixed it with blue velvet ribbon, the same sort that edged his lapels and cuffs. "As I was telling your aunt, I have a great deal to atone for when it comes to you, Miss Stewart."

Insistent, I said, "No, of course you don't . . ."

"I think I do," he replied, and tried to catch my gaze.

Panic clutched at my heart and stilled it. In my mind, I all but bargained with possibility. He couldn't have come all this way to court me — that was madness, wasn't it?

Even if his coach trip from Skeleton Ranch to West Glory had been entirely uneventful, it was still a journey of significant hardship and distance, to come from Maryland to Oklahoma Territory. Surely he'd meant to come this way on his own. Certainly it was a coincidence that he stopped at my aunt's homestead . . .

Then, to destroy my anxious hope, Theo said, "I have only the most honorable intentions."

I looked at the ground, and my vision blurred. The last thing I wanted were his *intentions*. My love lay in the cold ground, forever sleeping beneath the flowering pear trees, and that's where it would stay.

Words were dust in my mouth when I said, "You're too kind."

"Where will you be staying?" Birdie asked.

"I've got a room in town for now. The school board said they'd help me find a modest place of my own as soon as they could."

At that, I lifted my head. "Will they? Is that common?"

Theo smiled, offering me his card. "Common enough, I suppose. I'm taking the schoolmaster post in West Glory."

Once again, my manners failed. "Why would you do that?"

Tipping his hat, Theo smiled once more—as if he hadn't noticed my discomfit at all. In fact, his black eyes sparkled, dancing as if he'd met a particularly toothsome challenge. "As I said, I have only the most honorable intentions."

With that, he mounted his very fine horse and made his pretty adieus to Birdie and Louella. They watched him go, for he was quite something to consider, but I studied his calling card instead.

It was one of the most fashionable kinds. The front bore his name, and on the reverse, each corner had a word printed in it. Instead of scribbling a note, he simply had to fold the corner that best expressed his sentiment, so it would appear on the face. Today, he'd presented *Visite*, as if I might not have noticed that he'd delivered it in person.

The paper was so thick, it weighed in my palm, and I knew those extra engravings came at quite a fee. This wasn't the card of a poet at all; it belonged, instead, to a very rich man. In a moment, all my assumptions about him shifted.

And they made him seem rather more dangerous to me, a wastrel for entertainment's sake, a rich boy used to getting what he wanted. I couldn't bear to think what that meant; I refused to consider that I might be the thing he wanted.

"I see?" Louella asked, pulling my hand down so she could grasp for the card.

"You may keep it," I told her, and went to collect my wash.

To my dismay, Theo's visit lit a fire in my Aunt Birdie. While I tried to master the temperamental woodstove, she finished the last of her lacework with a giddy sort of amusement.

"Can't feature running away from that," she said as I handed Louella a pan of peas to pick.

Clasping the back of my neck, I avoided Birdie's gaze and turned back to the stove. "It's not what you think at all."

.I started chopping my field onions, rough, hard strokes to work out the tension between my shoulder blades. My plan was to mix them with the cornmeal, to make a flavored cornbread, just a touch of variety to go with boiled, mashed peas.

"That boy is a sugar cake," Birdie said. Amused, she raised her lace to inspect it and spoke to me through it. "Melt right on your tongue."

My gaze flew to Louella, who had not the slightest idea what kind of conversation was flying around her little curly head. She'd centered the pan of peas between her legs. Her face had transformed, a mask of concentration, as she picked the pods open one by one.

Satisfied that Louella was unaware, I nevertheless lowered my voice before replying. "Do you know where I met him? At the cemetery. Drinking in the daylight, sharing a toast with a dead poet."

This revelation further delighted Birdie at my expense. "So he cuts a dramatic figure."

"A foolish one," I replied.

"Obviously, it intrigued you enough to meet him at the dance." Birdie folded her lace carefully, then leaned back in the chair to appraise me. "And into the gardens . . ."

Rather harder than I meant to, I dropped a pan on the

stovetop. "In both cases, he followed me. In both cases, I fled."

"That's not what Pauline said in her letter."

I swept around, dropping to the floor. I clapped my hands over Louella's ears, which didn't seem to bother her at all. Apparently, she had found her bliss in a handful of peas.

"It's not that way at all. I left him with my friend, and that would have been the last of it if I hadn't fallen in the fountain! He didn't ravish *me,* I ravished *him* so Mama would . . . what's so funny?"

Birdie covered her mouth, rolling her eyes heavenward. And she shook, loose curls dancing around her face, reminding me how young — how pretty — she was.

"What?" I demanded again.

She shook with one more giggle. Then she made note of my furious scowl and put a hand out to pet me. "Shhh, shhh, Zora . . ."

Still furious, I shrugged from beneath her hand. "There's no romance there."

"It seems like there could be," Birdie said. She leveled me with a look. "If you say you keep running, but this boy keeps turning up, maybe the Lord is trying to tell you something."

It seemed to me that the Lord surely had more things to worry about than one new spinster in Oklahoma Territory.

But I didn't say that. I got up and went back to the stove, turning all my attention to my onion cornbread.

Her voice more serious, Birdie said, "I know what it's like to lose your heart, Zora."

"I haven't lost it." A knot bound my throat, and I had to blink fast to keep from salting the cakes with my tears. "It's Thomas' still, and I'd like to stop talking about this."

Birdie stood and smoothed a hand across my shoulders. She patted me gently and leaned in to murmur, "All right. For now."

As determined as she was to delay this conversation, inwardly I killed it entirely. If she spoke on it again, I'd ignore her. She was barely my elder, twenty-two to my seventeen, so I couldn't outright defy her. But I could hold my tongue and had done so for months in my mother's house.

Perhaps I would become another Wild West notion, a legend sent back east in the newspapers. Zora Stewart, the mute keeper of Thomas Rea's memory, first mourning lady of the plains, raiser of other women's children.

It did not occur to me at that moment that I might in fact become part of the mythic West for something else entirely. But soon it would, and I would wonder if the Lord or the universe had, in fact, led me to this place apurpose.

I felt no sense of destiny in myself, but my feelings would hardly deter fate.

Come the morning, Birdie woke me before the sun had entirely risen. Pressing a finger to her lips, she motioned for me to follow her. Tugging a blanket around my shoulders, I slipped outside, leaving Louella sleeping peacefully on her pallet.

"I'm heading into town," Birdie said.

She wore a green calico dress, the perfect shade to bring out the color in her eyes. Tying on her good bonnet—the ironed one that spent most of its time on a peg—she nodded in the vague direction of West Glory. "I should be back by lunch, but if it's not 'til supper, don't worry."

Worry tightened my skin. "You don't want me to hurry and dress Louella? We could come along."

"I'll get more done more quickly if you stay behind."

I wanted to be agreeable, so I nodded. But I struggled for words, my mind whirring. I had my tasks for the day, and they were no different than they would have been if Birdie were going to be here. But somehow, minding the baby and the stove seemed less daunting with her nearby.

Taking my silence for agreement, Birdie said, "Put on a happy face. I'll be paid today, and that means a bit of meat for our beans and, if we're very lucky, some flour and sugar. I'll bring you a penny candy if you're good."

Sheepishly, I laughed. "I favor cinnamons."

"You'll get whatever Mrs. Herrington has at the general." Birdie put her hands on my shoulders, her freckled face turning more serious. "If there's any trouble, bar the door and keep the shotgun at hand."

"I can't," I said bluntly.

Birdie mistook my meaning. "It's already loaded. Just raise it to your shoulder and pull the trigger if you have to. It's unlikely, Zora. Before Mr. de la Croix, we hadn't had a visitor since . . . well, since the funeral, and that's a year past."

"I'm sorry," I said; my condolences came without thought, as if grief were written into my bones now.

"Don't be." Birdie picked up her basket of sewing. Then she fixed me with a quelling stare. "Just tell me you understand and you'll take care of my Lou."

There was no need to argue with her. Truly, if no one came here, then handling arms would be no issue. And if someone did come, I'd devise another way to protect Louella—if she needed protecting at all. So I covered my lie of omission with a truth.

"As if she were my own."

"Good girl," Birdie said, turning to start the long walk to town. She laughed lightly, casting a look back over her shoulder. "You might get that penny candy yet."

After breakfast, I drew our morning water and went out back to tend the garden.

I recognized most of the vegetables there—the peas were the most obvious, because they had already shed their blossoms to produce their fruit. Long, leafy blades marked the row of corn, and beside that, two sad tomato plants withered on their stakes.

There were vines that I guessed would become pumpkins, and green tufts flush to the ground that would surely become carrots. Birdie claimed there were Irish potatoes and onions down there too, but I saw no evidence.

"Do you know what's funny?" I asked Louella as she squatted in the pea row to pick the ripe pods. "My mama has a garden just like this one at home. Smaller, but everything's in the same order. Can you believe it?"

Louella looked up from her pan. "Your mama knows my mama?"

"Yes! My mama is your Aunt Pauline."

Considering this, Louella sat down in the dirt. "My mama's Beatrice."

I smiled, carrying my bucket to the outside basin, dipping the last of the water up for the possibly imaginary onions. "I know."

"My name's Louella." She pulled another pea, holding it up to the sunlight. The thin skin glowed green, the shadow of peas nestled inside it. "Louella. And Aldith. And Neal. I have three names."

Though I'm sure I'd heard her whole name at one time or another, it delighted me to have her put it all together. "Our grandmother's name was Aldith. You're named for her."

"Is she dead?"

Putting the bucket back on its hook, I went over to pick her up. "Yes. A long time ago, before you were ever born."

"Oh. Did she get sick?"

Stroking her darling curls, I shook my head. "No, duck. She'd lived her entire life, and it was over, that's all."

Louella curled an arm around my neck. "My papa died."

She said it as easily as I would have said *The sky is blue* or *You're three years old*. My heart ached, because a year must have seemed like a very long time ago indeed to such a little girl. But another pang came, not for grief but Louella's curious lack of it.

"Yes, he did," I finally agreed.

Louella moved on easily. "Let's go on a 'venture."

Relieved, I carried her back to the house. Those peas needed to go inside, and I had to consider her request. Without committing myself to anything in particular, I asked, "What kind of adventure?"

Louella shrugged, waiting for me to make the plans.

While I put the peas away, I wondered if there was a single adventuresome thing to do nearby, and couldn't think of one. Well, besides chasing the chickens, and it was my sworn duty to get Louella to leave them in peace.

My gaze fell on the shotgun beside the door, and I shivered. Well, the best way to avert trouble at the soddy would be to leave it, I supposed. "Come on outside. Let me see what I can find."

Taking my hand, Louella stood beside me as I peered toward the horizon. The dust had risen again, hazing the world, but I wasn't looking for something with my regular sight. I breathed deep, searching inside myself for the earth's pulse, waiting to taste the clarity of nearby water on my tongue.

Whispering, Louella rubbed my hand against her face. "Whatcha doing?"

"Shhh," I said.

I felt a bit foolish, straining to see something that should have been beyond my gaze. What if I'd imagined everything? What if this really was a touch of lingering madness, a way to keep my dear, departed friend in my heart?

Thinking about it in daylight, it seemed quite rational that I would hallucinate an affinity to water. It made me not the opposite of Amelia's fire as I'd supposed, but her salvation. She had seen in fire and succumbed to the heat of a fever. If I had been water then, I could have saved her. However late my fantasy, it was made to save her.

I had very nearly talked myself out of the search when I caught sight of a glimmering in the grass. In the daylight, the threads of water weren't nearly so easy to pick out. But they were there, and once more, I could feel them fanning across the prairie, the blood in this earthly flesh.

"This way," I said, tugging Louella along. "We're going wading."

~~~~~~~

Louella dropped into the grass, a little rag doll with no bones at all. Though her point was quite clear, she felt it necessary to explain. "Tired, Zora."

The stream that seemed so very nearby when it was a light on the horizon was nearly two miles off by my best guess. Butterflies and pretty flowers had ceased to amuse Louella, and now I was stuck. I could drag her the rest of the way and *then* home again, or just home again.

As if to decide for me, a haunting cry filled the air. A low, musical moan surrounded me, and the hair stood up on my arms. It sounded very like the melody Papa had taught me to make by blowing in a conch shell. But there was no sea-shore here. And the lowing sounded all around us.

"Up, Lou," I said, grabbing her arm.

Instead of rising up, she resisted. A wobbling weight on the end of my wrist, Louella showed no concern about the eerie call that encircled us. My skin stung with cold—a frost come early. How could she be so carefree? I picked her up forcibly.

Old fear fed new. The men who robbed the stagecoach, what if they'd been watching—waiting to catch me alone to finish me off? What if I had wandered onto someone else's land or stumbled into an ancient burying ground?

A black geist flew at me. It was a beating wave of dark, and two furious orange sparks for eyes. I screamed. The hollow note of it rang on and on, but I wasn't entirely use-less. I struck the phantasm. Then I scrambled back, drag-ging Louella with me. In my sudden strength, she felt light as feathers.

Feathers.

"You hit the birdie," Louella said. She giggled, laying her head on my shoulder.

And, dear God, I had.

Though my heart still roared, my head filled with sheep-ish realization. At my feet, a large bird staggered. It looked rather like a primordial chicken. Its feathers were black and gold striped, with bright, burnished spots on either side of its head.

It reeled drunkenly and made a sound I could best describe as a crackling. And in that instant, I didn't see a poor creature in want of care and deliverance. I saw supper: fried chicken, or stewed; roasted or barbecued. Something savory to make up for a week of beans and peas and cold beans and cold peas.

Sliding Louella to her feet, I leaned to whisper in her ear, "Don't go far, but see if you can find a nest."

This was a better adventure than walking to eternity, and she immediately dashed into the prairie. Which left me alone to suck up my courage to wring the bird's neck without an impressionable witness.

I was kind and quick as I could be about it, and all I wished for was a good piece of twine to make a brace for carrying it home.

"Eggs," Louella shouted. "Zora, eggs!"

Taking my prize along, I followed the sound of her voice and found her crouched over a little nest built in the grass. It held ten fat eggs, each the color of toasted meringue. Quickly, I took in the land around us—there was no hen nearby, though I heard a new conch-wail in the distance.

"Take four," I told Louella. One for each of us, and one

for the pot. That was my thinking on it, and it left six for the bereaved hen I'd likely just widowed. "Gather up your skirt and carry them gently."

She did as I told her, and it was only halfway back to the soddy that she turned her face up at me. "No wading?"

"I'm afraid not," I told her. And as the wind rushed through the sunbaked prairie, I had to laugh at myself. It was no desert, this piece of the Territories, but it was no oasis, either.

I had been a mad, impetuous thing to promise her wading at all. Still, considering our reward for my madness, I was glad to take the blow to my ego.

A hot dinner tonight! A hot breakfast tomorrow! We were rich!

Seven

The next day, I felt rather less wealthy when I made Louella's hot breakfast and Aunt Birdie still hadn't come home. Her promise to return by supper at the latest had slipped into dusk, then into the night, with no sign of her.

It was frighteningly easy to lie to the baby, to coax her to sleep. But it was impossible for me to find sleep myself.

I kept going into the yard, peering into the dark for any sign of my wayward aunt. My head cried with unfortunate possibilities, one worse than the next. Finally, though I knew candles and oil were dear, I lit the tin lantern and left it outside to be a beacon.

By morning, the oil was gone, and we were still alone. Louella smacked her spoon against her breakfast, not a bite of egg passing her lips. She drew her head back like a turtle, her chin disappearing into her neck, and her eyes nothing but sullen green dots that followed me as I straightened the soddy.

"You need to eat, duck," I told her, folding up our bedding. I stole peeks at her over the top of the quilt. "It's a long walk to the well."

She answered with another smack of her spoon.

I continued, cheerfully. "And we might have another adventure today. You never know. You'll want a full belly for that."

Eyes darkening, Louella said nothing. But she kicked the legs of the chair, making eggs dance in her plate and filling the soddy with a sharp, steady beat. I kept to my chores, hoping this tempest would pass as quickly as any of her moods.

When I gave her no response, she kicked harder, making the chair rock. I turned my back to her, surprised by the great well of temper that filled me. Every thump reverberated on my spine. The tap of the tin spoon on her plate dug right into my ear.

Ignoring her, it seemed, made the tantrum worse. Slowly, I put the bedding away and collected myself. I would be calm in the face of this obstinance. Turning toward her, I pasted on a smile. "Now let's finish —"

But I didn't finish.

She kicked so hard that the plate leapt from her knees. It was impressive that she managed to break Birdie's only china plate on a dirt floor. It was infuriating, too. I would have eaten that breakfast gladly. I might have even picked it off the floor, if it weren't full of shards.

I flew over to remonstrate, pointing at the mess. "Look what you've done! That plate is ruined!"

Louella's mercury turned. She looked up at me, stricken, and burst into tears. And though I had only raised my voice to her—in truth, wished very much to shake her, but resisted—she tried to climb into my arms for comfort.

Taking her up, I smoothed my hand over her hair, letting her soak my neck with the slick effluvia of her tears. What an awful, cruel thing I had become.

Crooning to her, I choked on a sob of my own, then cut it off viciously. The wideness of the plains had never seemed more desolate to me, but I had no right to cry.

My fears were stupid and childish—if someone had set on Birdie, I wouldn't be left alone in the prairie with a baby.

I'd take her home to Baltimore, where Mama would know how to make her eat a plate of eggs without shouting. I'd have a clean dress and a corset, hot meals thrice daily, and water that ran from a pump in the kitchen again.

"Shhh, shhh," I whispered to Louella, rocking her, though she had stopped crying in earnest. I rocked her so hard, it seemed the earth floor trembled beneath us. "We'll sweep it all up. It's no matter at all."

Suddenly, someone knocked on the door, and Louella started in my arms. "Mama!" she cried, wriggling free and running to throw the door open. But the shape in the doorway frightened her, and she ran back to my skirts.

"Mr. Birch," I said.

He was so tall he had to lean a bit to see inside, his broad shoulders casting a wide shadow. I stepped in front of him, ashamed to let him see the terrible mess Lou and I had made of the house. "To what do I owe the pleasure?"

Tipping his hat back, he looked from Louella to me and asked, "Where's your aunt?"

"In town," I said airily. "She'll be along anytime now."

"I brought you something."

Then he turned and walked away, an invitation to follow him. This time I did, for it was a relief to see proof that we weren't forgotten out on Plot 325.

Louella kept one arm tight around my neck. "Who is?" she asked around her finger.

"A friend," I told her.

Emerson strode to his buckboard and lifted a parcel from

it. When he turned, I realized it was my muddied silk scarf, and it hung heavy with something wrapped in it. Instead of simply handing it to me, he cradled it in his arm and folded back the corners.

Peppers. Dark green capsicum peppers, nestled beside two fat tomatoes and a striped turnip, on a bed of white and yellow corn. He shifted the pack, to give account of its contents. "Some beans and some onions, too. I wanted to bring carrots, but they weren't ready yet."

My mouth watered, but I hesitated. "I haven't got any money. I lost everything on the coach."

Emerson tied the bundle, then handed it to Louella, who didn't know any better than to take it. "I don't have any money either. That's for the well."

"I . . . all right."

With a deep breath, he started to speak but thought better of it. He tipped his hat to Louella, then to me, making as if to take to his buckboard again.

At that, I should have said thank you and bid him goodbye. But he seemed full, round with some kind of anticipation. Against my own best judgment, I wanted to uncover it.

"Wait! May I ask you a question, Mr. Birch?"

He smiled at that, a crooked tilt to his lips. "Why so formal, Miss Stewart?"

I hefted Louella up on my hip and lifted my chin. "It's not formal, it's polite. You have *heard* of manners, haven't you?"

"I was thinking I might ask you the same thing."

His gaze trailed from mine, and he made the oddest expression—eyes rounded and nose pinched. I realized he was trying to make Louella laugh. Warmth flooded my skin, touching me with an unexpected fondness.

Nuzzling against Louella's hair, I gave her a little kiss, then asked, "How do you make your garden grow so prettily? Ours is struggling."

Rubbing his hands together, he seemed to ponder the question. Then he met my eyes again. There was no mistaking it, not in moonlight or sunshine: he was very handsome and not the least bit affected. I wondered what he saw when he looked at me.

He interrupted my vanity with a question. "Can I take a look?"

Honestly, I should have told him no. My little mourning Zora protested, and I knew Birdie wouldn't be happy to have had him near her home at all. But I was hungry and lonely . . . and perhaps the slightest bit fascinated.

So I said yes.

With long strides, Emerson marked the boundary of Aunt Birdie's garden. He said nothing but occasionally made a small sound. Thoughtful, like a doctor giving examination to a broken arm. Thomas sometimes hummed like that —

I buried the thought. It made my throat tight, and I simply didn't want to taste bittersweet on my tongue at that moment. Putting Louella on her feet, I gave her a pat to send her to play.

Instead, she decided to shadow Emerson. Aping his steps, she lifted her foot so high, I thought she might fall backwards, but no. She marched after him, a little goose who still hadn't had her breakfast.

"It could use more water," he began.

I tried not to groan. Leaning against the house, the yoke taunted me, its buckets sitting empty as an indictment. "All right."

Finally, Emerson crouched at the row of corn. Sunlight caught in his hair, casting threads of bronze through the dark gold mess of it. "The tomatoes would be happier if the corn weren't casting shadows on them."

Rubbing the heat from my cheek, I nodded, as if I understood the first thing about a vegetable's pleasure. "My mother's garden is laid out the same way."

"North facing?" He asked. And I realized it was an explanation. Unlike Mama's, Birdie's garden took shade from the house in the morning and apparently shade from the corn in the afternoon.

So I said, "Too late to change that now."

He nodded. Then he turned to Louella, who'd crouched beside him in the same posture. "Can you keep a secret?"

"Oh yessss."

"And do you believe in magic?"

Her mouth a little O, Louella was too excited to speak. Instead, she nodded, her curls bobbing merrily.

Emerson raised his eyes to mine, asking the same question with a look. And it was strange, our gazes connecting like that. A tremor passed beneath my feet, and I realized with a shock, I had felt it before. When he'd come upon me in the dark. And again, just before I'd answered the door.

It was him.

My magic reacted in his proximity. Suddenly, all the water I had struggled to seek the day before rose easily, silver lines that shone like dew, spread out all around us. When my eyes met his, he simply raised his brows. Waiting yet for an answer, though I felt certain that he knew.

Thus, finding my voice, I said, "I continue to marvel at your flair for the dramatic, Mr. Birch."

"Marvel away," he told me. Then he rubbed his fingers in the loose earth before him. Wriggling them beneath the soil, he took a long, deep breath.

The wind shifted, but did nothing to ward off my sudden chill. I'd seen that same smoothing of a face before, felt that same eerie calm of connection in Amelia as I'd watched her make prophecies.

But this time, instead of a scrap of writing or just a spoken word, there were wonders to be *seen*. Little, curled leaves stretched, the plants before me shivering, waking—growing. Delicate yellow blossoms burst forth on the tomatoes; the corn suddenly realized its ambition and climbed toward the sky.

"Magic," Louella whispered.

And if she saw it too, then it was real. It was all real. My knees weakened, and my heart took the queerest turn. Not until this summer past had my life been anything but ordinary. Spoiled, but ordinary. And now . . .

"Now," Emerson said, breaking the spell. He brushed his hands off and stood, as if most farmers simply willed their crops to grow. "They need more water. Four times a day, every day."

"I'll make sure they get it." Shaking myself to my senses, I crooked a finger at Louella. But I wouldn't hold my curiosity. Without guile, without shyness, I asked Emerson, "How did you learn to do this?"

He nodded, following Louella back to me. "You first."

.My throat closed. What could I possibly say that wouldn't sound entirely mad? And yet, had he not just coaxed an entire garden to life? Had he not bared his gift to me, in exactly the way I had? The only difference was that I hadn't realized what I was doing until it was done.

So I softened, imploring, "Please, Mr. Birch."

And it seemed he understood me. Voice lowered, as if confiding, he bowed his head toward mine.

"On accident. Pa went off to work the railroad and left us with nothing a whole summer. Said I was the man of the house and I had to look after things, so I did. I made the garden grow." He shrugged, his eyes darting to look past me. "My ma said I had a green thumb, but it's a whole lot more than that, I'd say."

"Quite an understatement." Laughter slipped out of me in strange relief. He'd *needed* the earth to move for him, and it had. Just as I'd needed the water to show itself. I couldn't help but wonder what Amelia had needed, to bring her visions from the fires.

I brushed that thought aside and made myself smile again. Looking up at Emerson, I said, "But it does make sense to bring such a gift to the land rush."

A slight darkness crossed his brow. "That was the idea, anyhow. Didn't work out like I expected."

"Whatever do you mean?"

"Exactly what I said." Banishing his darkness with his own smile, he turned the conversation on me."All right. Now, how about you? You always been a springsweet?"

The word spilled on my skin, clean and clear. I rolled it in my thoughts, longed to roll it on my tongue. Should I have thought to call myself anything, it would have been a dowser. Or a water witch. Somehow, his name for it made it seem rather more enchanted.

Picking Louella up, I said, "Well, you see—I'd been rescued by a cad in the middle of the night, and I wanted to put him in his place with a grand show. To my surprise, it worked—and he was entirely impressed with me. All but called me his goddess."

Feigning ignorance, he fought back a smile. "When was that? It'd have to be before we met."

Refusing to dignify that with a reply, I started for the front of the house. "You really should go before Birdie gets back. She's already overdue."

I felt him following me, my senses stirring with awareness. It was nothing supernatural; no, it was something far more usual. He amused me; I liked his company.

Just to prove his charming, prickly difference, he brushed past then turned to walk backwards before me. "Now who's forgetting their manners?"

"Please," Louella chirped. Of course, she had no idea why. She'd simply learned that if someone prompted her about manners, she was missing one of the important sweetening words.

Holding her close, my darling anchor, I said, "Thank you, Mr. Birch. For everything. We've been hungry, to be honest. Your gifts are much appreciated."

Softening, Emerson stepped up on his buckboard and tipped his hat to me. "It's a pleasure, Miss Stewart." Then he tipped it to Louella. "Good day, Miss Neal."

"Gooday," Louella replied brightly.

Though he took the reins in his hands, Emerson hesitated. And then he looked to me. His eyes weren't golden, not as I'd thought. They were like skies and summer wheat—shades of blue and green and gold woven together. And his gaze direct seemed to mark my skin. "Hope I see you again."

I couldn't find my voice, and he gave me no chance to deny him. With a crack of leather, Epona was off, the buckboard trailing dust like smoke. Raising Louella's hand, I helped her wave goodbye, and soon Emerson was nothing more than a faint shadow on the horizon.

And for the sparest moment, I wished him back.

At last, Birdie opened the front door, popping her head in and singing, "Who wants a cinnamon?"

I leapt up, excitement and relief setting me free. My aunt was well, and home again. And her face seemed brighter than it had before, her eyes dancing and her smile wide.

Throwing herself into her mother's arms, Louella opened her mouth and spilled out two entire days in a confused jumble. "We went wading, and eggs, and SO much water, but the plate is broke and Zora says we can get a new one, I'm sorry, and . . ."

Birdie wrapped Louella up in her arms and her skirts. She dropped a kiss on her brow and her nose, murmuring motherly things to her that I couldn't quite make out. They needed no real translation; she was glad to be home and to see her babe again.

"Where have you been?" I asked, pressing against the ache in my chest.

Birdie looked to me, her smile turning impish. "I'll tell you all about it just as soon as you help me carry in the groceries."

"Yes, of course," I said. I rubbed her arm as I went by, just a touch to tell her I was glad she'd returned. I wanted to be a child and demand an answer immediately. But I didn't have to, for when I stepped into the yard, there stood Theo.

He leaned against a brand-new phaeton—parked just far

enough away that I'd missed the chiming of its brass fittings from inside the soddy.

I knew it to be brand-new because the rims of its wheels shone with scarlet varnish, and the dust had barely hazed the black footboard. It matched him exactly: his dark hair and the red pansy pinned in his buttonhole.

"Mr. de la Croix," I murmured.

"Miss Stewart," he replied. And then he turned to lift a wooden box from the phaeton's floor. Carrying it toward me, he tried to coax a smile from me. "There's a pretty color in your cheeks today."

Turning inwardly, I put my attention on the groceries, instead of his face. "You're very kind. Especially to bring my aunt home all this way. This would have been quite a burden to carry."

"After the trouble in town, I couldn't bear to let her come all this way unescorted."

So I had been right to worry; afraid for good reason, it seemed! I dropped the packet of sugar I was inspecting and asked, "What trouble?"

Theo tried to soothe me with a smile. "It's only a bit of unpleasantness that's done; would you dwell on it?"

Singed by a flare of heat, I drew myself up. Though quite a bit shorter than Theo, I could still meet his eye by deliberation. I didn't care to be handled as if I were a child.

I'd kept the truth from Louella for good reason—I'd known nothing for certain and there was little point in upsetting a babe. Nevertheless, Theo had no right to keep the truth from *me*. "I assure you, Mr. de la Croix, once you tell me, I shan't."

To his credit, he realized he'd erred. Putting the box on the ground, he rose to put a hand on my shoulder and lean in confidentially. "The post office was robbed yesterday noon. Fortunately, Mrs. Neal had collected her packages before the fact. Unfortunately, after the fact, the marshal wanted everyone to stay indoors until he could conduct his investigation."

My belly stirred, a nervous flutter. "Was anyone hurt?"

"No, though I understand quite a few mailbags suffered mortal wounds," Theo said, then straightened to stand a more respectable distance from me. He gazed at me from beneath his dark lashes, though, the faintest touch of flirtatiousness in his expression. "It was invigorating, to tell the truth. Nothing so exciting ever happened in Baltimore."

It was not his fault he said exactly the wrong thing to me. And I tried very hard to keep that in mind. I supposed that to someone who'd never suffered it, gunfire in the street might be very *invigorating* indeed.

Trying to rein my temper, I snatched the groceries up and said, "Well, it was good of you to see Birdie home."

"You know it was to see you," he said, a plaintive note following me as I turned to go inside.

Closing my eyes, I stood there and waited for some kind of peace to come over me. Then I turned to face him. "Mr. de la Croix, what I did at the Sugarcane Ball was inexcusable, and I apologize most profusely . . ."

Theo held up a hand to stay me. "If you would, please, just let me plead my case. I've watched you for months, Miss Stewart. There are only so many drinks a man can have with cold stone before he is labeled, quite understandably, a fop. I did not go to Westminster for Mr. Poe; I went for you."

It was such a strange and ardent confession that, I admit, I felt nothing at all in that moment but confusion. Perhaps I should have apologized again and made my leave, but my tongue always had run ahead of me. "You do understand I wasn't there to make rubbings and collect flowers."

Pressing a hand to his chest, Theo approached me again. He was porcelain sincerity, his composure as artfully broken as Miss Austen could have ever done it. "I am so very sorry for the loss of your Mr. Rea."

"Thank you," I said stiffly.

He went on. "Please know, Miss Stewart, I didn't follow you to the ball, I was there anyway. When I saw you come in, I thought, well, I had assumed —"

"That my mourning was over."

"Precisely." Now he cured his posture, perhaps uncomfortable in how bare he'd laid himself. Glancing away, he cleared his throat, then finally met me again. "I tell you again, with every sentiment in me, that my intentions toward you are honorable."

There was a reason, I suppose, that in Baltimore we did so much courting by notes and cards and chaperoned dances. It was hard to speak directly, to risk your feelings or to spare others theirs. The knot in my throat only tightened. "It's no defect of yours, Mr. de la Croix, but I can't imagine that I will ever love anyone again."

"I wouldn't ask you to," he said. "But do you suppose you could grow to like me?"

I didn't answer, and I suppose preferring to take silence as possibility, Theo climbed into his phaeton. Selfishly, I was glad that I would see him go, but Birdie hurried into the yard before he could.

"Don't go," she said, dropping a hand on my shoulder. "I owe you a dinner at the very least."

Taking up the black leather reins, which had been stained to match the horse and the phaeton, Theo tipped his head toward her. "It's late yet, and I have to finish studying for my certificate. But I do thank you for the invitation."

Birdie nodded. "Why don't you come back tomorrow? You could take Zora for a ride."

Theo's attention drifted toward me, and I burned. It was awful to be caught this way, to have no graceful way to decline. And to make it worse, Birdie dug her fingers into my shoulder a bit, waiting for a response.

"It *is* a handsome buggy," I said. It was the best I could manage, both polite and noncommittal.

With a smile, Theo said, "Yes, I should like that," and only then did Birdie set me free.

~~~~~~~~

Whipping a bit of sugar and flour into a bowl of cornmeal, Birdie shook all over. It was far more effort than she needed expend to make a simple batter, and it was obvious from the hard plane of her brow that she was cross.

I was likewise irritated at her meddling, so it was for the best. She would torment her batter, and I would mind the stew—made with the last of our roasted chicken.

Picking through Emerson's vegetables, I chose the turnip to peel next. I didn't care for them, and if chopped small enough, they'd only taste of stew, which suited me. I was halfway through skinning the awful, biting thing when I realized Birdie had stopped stirring.

"What's that?" she asked.

She waved a battered spoon in my direction. And before I could say a word, Louella offered from the floor, "Mr. Birch's turnips."

"Oh," Birdie said, her tone thoroughly sugared for the baby's sake, the message quite sharp for mine. "They're Mr. Birch's turnips? Did they knock on the door?"

Louella laughed, rolling onto her back. "Silly mama!"

Still paring the turnips, I steadied myself to interject. I kept my tone quite still, weighing each word before I spoke. "He brought them when he returned my scarf."

The cracking of Birdie's façade was coming. She put her bowl aside and pulled Louella to her feet. Birdie sent her outside to count the corn, a useless task that I wasn't sure she could complete. But it did get her out of the soddy before her mother lost her temper.

"Didn't I tell you —"

"I didn't invite him," I said, quick to my own defense. "He came of his own accord."

Birdie snatched her wooden spoon up again, and for an irrational moment, I thought she might strike me with it. But instead, she attacked her batter, dropping thick dollops of it into sizzling grease. "You don't seem to understand the gravity of your situation, little miss."

"What? What situation? I'm here, aren't I? Don't I mind the baby? Don't I do everything you ask of me?"

"Not everything, obviously."

I choked on the unfairness of it. Tossing the turnip into my pot, I reached for another prize from Emerson's bundle, a fine, fat potato to slice before Birdie's very eyes. "I thanked him, and he left. And it would have been just the same if you'd been here."

"Bad enough the boy's a sooner." Another round of batter hit the grease with a wheeze. "Bad enough he snatched up good land that he's already got growing! Bad enough he does all his trading in Jubilee just to rile those fat-headed fools in West Glory! We don't need borrowed trouble, Zora Pauline. Times are hard enough for the Neals, thank you."

My frustration overflowed. "I don't know what any of that means!"

Putting the bowl down hard, Birdie turned to me. "It means you're another mouth I have to feed because you went wild back home. The least you could do is make that easy on me."

The insinuation felt like oil running down my spine, leaving me slick and filthy. Mustering as much dignity as I could, I refused to let her believe me ashamed. "Haven't

I? We're having fresh tomatoes, and stew that's more than boiled bean water tonight because I dowsed a well for Mr. Birch."

Birdie halted. "Excuse me?"

"I dowsed a well for him; he paid me in green goods!"

"You did no such thing."

Throwing my hands out, I demanded, "Why would I make something like that up? After what happened last summer, why would I *ever* claim something like that if it weren't true?"

The air cooled; Birdie deflated. She said nothing for a long moment, turning the corn cakes over in their grease. Something stirred across her face, a light or a thought, one that touched her brow just so. One that set her eyes to flickering as she stared at our supper.

Uneasy, I said, "Birdie?"

Finally, she replied. "Show me."

~~~~~~~

Arms crossed tight against her chest, Birdie peered into the prairie. "Petty had to dig us three wells. The first one came up dry. The second one collected water but didn't fill up the way it should. We're using the third one now."

I felt as though someone had tightened a hot ribbon around my throat. "I see."

"Go on, Zora." Birdie's eyes pierced me. There was a hunger to them, an edge that reminded me she'd had ever so many more thin and cold meals than I had. "If you can dowse proper, everything changes for us. Show me. Where's my second well?"

Trembling against the sharpness of her hunger, I took a single step and looked into the fields. Gold chased green, an endless ripple of grasses until the horizon. With the day near-ended, dust hung in the air. It separated us from the other homesteads, rubbing away any hint that we were anything but alone on the prairie.

Uncertain, I closed my eyes and listened to the wind. To the whisper of bowing grain and the hum of bees wandering nearby. Beneath that, the crackle of dry earth, the sudden hiss of dust thrown against the soddy's walls, there was water.

It came to me like a drumbeat, like a rhythm sustained. It was perfect, reverberating on my skin, ringing in my ears. And when I dared to look again, I saw a silver veil. It was delicate as dew and just as apt to dissipate. The brightest beads marked our everyday well, the one that ran pure and clean.

Turning from that, I followed the fainter strands. I moved, so suddenly that Birdie gasped, but I didn't stop to reassure her. I had no idea how long this connection would last; how certain my affinity could be. For a few paces, I walked, but then I hurried.

There was a spot quite near, one with a dull glimmer to it. I tasted brackish water, the way I'd tasted the rainwater in Emerson's well just by standing near it. Soon, my skirts cut through the grasses. The cotton snapped and whipped, my boots kicking still more dust into the already hazy air.

"Here!" I called, as the silver faded.

I pointed to a depression in the ground, rocks jutting through a layer of earth that was bald of any greenery.

Birdie stopped and bit her lower lip in silence. She wasn't worried; her brow was smooth. But her dark lashes fluttered, her eyes flickered: something was at work inside her head.

Softly, I said, "I'm right, aren't I?"

Clearing her throat, Birdie twisted to look at me. Instead of answering, she asked, "And you can do this anytime you like?"

"I don't know—yes, probably." I swallowed hard. "But how many wells do you need?"

It was a foolish question; Emerson Birch needed only one. Birdie Neal needed only one. But West Glory—and I'd discover soon, Jubilee—needed many, many more. Every homesteader needed water for survival.

That's what Birdie meant when she said everything would change. She saw only the possibility, only the promise of a better life in a desolate land. But standing there, over a dead well that I had ascertained by magic alone, she couldn't fathom just how *much* would change.

I could, but I let it happen anyway.

Eight

Birdie woke me early, coaxing me carefully out of bed to keep from waking Louella.

Bleary, I followed her outside. The sky was still dark, just beginning to glow in the east. Cool without my shawl, I wrapped my arms around myself and followed her to the back. We hadn't discussed my gift since I'd proved it the day before; I wondered if she'd blocked it out entirely.

Especially when she produced two buckets I'd never seen, blackened on the inside and graying on the out. I took the one she handed to me, peering down into it. "Did you want me to fetch water?"

"I've got some. Stuff the bottom of that with some straw, and don't lose the stopper."

Her instructions seemed like nonsense, and though I did as I was told, I had to ask, "What is this for?"

"Soaping," she said.

As the morning grew steadily brighter, my fog cleared. "I could go to town and fetch soap if you forgot it."

With a snort, Birdie said, "I'm not made of money, duck."

The little bag that she cut open puffed, as if it were full of smoke. But when she came closer, I realized it was full of ashes. My nose twitched when Birdie dumped it on top of the straw. Then she reached in after it, stirring it until pale, powdery tendrils rose up to be caught by the wind.

My ignorance must have shown, because Birdie took one look at me and said, "I'm not about to pay fifty cents for a pound of store-bought soap when I can get lard for a penny and wood ash for free."

What came after that was the most hideous chore I'd ever had the displeasure to complete. Making soap, I discovered, started with making lye.

Pulling the stopper from the ash bucket, Birdie told me to fill it with rainwater, slowly. I did, but the process seemed entirely useless—what could we possibly do with this?

But by some scientific miracle, the ash turned plain water to acid. It was foul stuff. It burned just to breathe its vapors, and though the cloudy liquid looked harmless enough, the slightest splash ate through cotton and flesh alike.

If I didn't know better, I would have believed Birdie picked soaping to both punish me for having Emerson on her land and to offer a contrast. Next to soaping, a ride with the devil would have been a delight. A ride with Theo de la Croix could only be ecstasy.

Late in the afternoon, Theo and his phaeton appeared in the distance to test that theory.

While I hurried to climb back into my corset, Birdie chatted with him in the yard. Her laughter rang through the oilpaper, bright and sweet. I laced myself breathless, listening to an impression of conversation. I heard no words at all, only voices. They rose and fell, fluidly matched. And there was a high color in Birdie's cheeks when I finally came out of the soddy.

"There she is," she sang, hefting Louella onto her hip.

I didn't meet Birdie's gaze, for I thought looking at her right then might spark my irritation again. To Theo, I said, "I apologize for keeping you."

"All is forgiven," Theo said, offering me his hand.

Handsome as ever, he wore a new suit. This one was shades of brown, with a frock coat cut to his knees and a cream silk ascot at his throat. He'd dispensed with the ribbon for his hair, so dark waves framed his face and carelessly brushed his shoulders. He would have been preciously fashionable in Baltimore. In Oklahoma Territory, he was too fine by half.

Louella strained at Birdie's arms. She reached for me—well, for the buggy. "I go?"

Leaning down for her, I was surprised when Birdie stepped back. Her nose brushed Louella's temple, and her eyes held mine as she said, "Next time, pet. This is a ride for big boys and girls."

"Shall we?" Theo asked as he settled beside me.

As I had no choice in the matter, I started to nod. Then it occurred to me—I would take the ride regardless of my wishes, but I alone could decide whether to enjoy it. So I smiled at Theo and at all the things this drive was: an escape from drudgery, a chance to talk to someone besides a toddler. "Let's do."

Newly bright, Theo snapped the reins and we took off. When I turned back to wave, Birdie had already hurried inside—she must have sprinted to disappear so quickly. I could make no sense of her, so I put her from my mind and didn't try at all.

I was amazed anew at how close the wilderness was. We'd driven barely ten minutes and yet found ourselves surrounded by open prairie and cloudless skies. The sun began its slow descent, making longer the plainness of the horizon.

Until then, we'd been quiet but for pleasantries. There was much to admire from the high seat of the phaeton, but as twilight settled, I forged our conversation so I could choose its direction. Hands laced together in my lap, I nodded toward the exquisite black mare and asked, "What's her name?"

Theo laughed sheepishly. Cutting a glance in my direction, he admitted, "Annabel Lee."

"So you *are* a fan of Mr. Poe's," I said.

With a toss of his head, he pretended indifference. "He is but one among many poets I admire. It's an exquisite calling, don't you think?"

"Writing verse?" I had never considered it, but it would've been rude to say that. Instead, I rearranged my shawl. "Since it drives men mad, it must be so. I've never heard of anyone wasting away on the sweet agony of figuring sums."

Theo startled me when he exclaimed, "Exactly! My father couldn't understand that. He thought I should dedicate myself to keeping the inventory for his company."

The slightest bit curious, I looked to him. "And what does your father do?"

"Shipping," Theo said. Just saying the word turned Theo's face sour, and he urged Annabel Lee to go a bit faster.

"You don't care for it?"

The wind pulled at Theo's hair, and he showed no signs

of slowing. "It's tedious, Miss Stewart. There are manifests forever going out, forever coming in. I couldn't care less about counting a thousand cases of olives or fifteen tons of coal or thirty-seven French hats with plumes."

"That does sound dull," I said. A particular lightness dared to flutter up in my chest—a faint tickle of relief. He'd come all this way to get from under his father's thumb, not to court me. "But won't you be taking it over someday? If I had shown the slightest inclination toward the law, my father would have made me partner straightaway."

With a distant smile, Theo shook his head. "I'm the second son, I'm afraid."

"My apologies," I said awkwardly.

"It's for the best. Here in the Territories, I can pen my own verses at night, and by day, it will be a pleasure to teach." Theo sounded quite genuine, as if he truly relished the opportunity to preside over a schoolroom instead of a boardroom. And then he doused my small lightness by saying, "And I should think this is a much more likely distance from which to catch your eye."

Dash propriety and manners; I twisted in the seat and looked up at him. "Tell me the truth, Mr. de la Croix. You didn't really come all this way to court me, did you?"

"You could call me Theo," he said.

When I didn't reply, he pulled the reins smoothly to stop

the horse. Suddenly still among the swaying grasses, the phaeton grew dreadfully quiet. But with more aplomb than I could have managed, Theo wound the reins round his hand and turned to me.

"The truth, Miss Stewart, is that I was leaving Baltimore regardless. Your flight simply encouraged my direction."

"And if I had stayed?"

Charming again, Theo waved a hand airily. "I would have written pathetic doggerel about your eyes and your mystery from an attic in Paris."

That made me smile, and I relaxed into the red velvet seat. "I tender my regrets to Calliope and all the muses for depriving them of your contributions."

"No doubt it weeps." He returned my smile, then added, "And I apologize for the unfortunate impression I may have left on your friend Miss Corey. She was eager to have me call until she realized I came to ask about you."

Ah, Mattie. I could imagine the smooth expression she must have effected; play-acting for suitors was one of her gifts. Straightening my skirts, I said, "Don't trouble yourself over it. You were but one dance, and she has Baltimore entirely to herself now."

We were, for a moment, comfortably quiet. And then Theo broke it by turning his gaze to the west. Red streaks of light played on his face, teasing through his hair. It darkened his lips, and his voice sank low when he murmured, "Have you ever seen such beautiful lights, Miss Stewart?"

Gently, to dissuade any romantic notion he might have about the moment, I said, "I'm afraid I don't care for sunsets anymore." It was the truth; a prophecy in the vespers had taken my Thomas from me.

But that was hardly Theo's fault, so I touched his shoulder lightly to turn his attention. "Do you think we could race a bit? I was enjoying it."

"It would be my pleasure," he replied. And in an instant, we were flying—away from the setting sun instead of toward it, into the welcoming velvet of night.

When I slept that night, I dreamt of sailing a measureless expanse of sea, the wind in my hair and light on my skin. But pity poor Mr. de la Croix, for in my dream I sailed with Emerson Birch at my side.

~~~~~~

As I had only driven it, I hadn't realized how long a walk it was to town. Starting early, with the morning still blooming, it was a pleasant trip. The stars flickered out one by one, swallowed when a pink sunrise chased away the night.

Louella actually slept in the basket of a little wagon that Birdie and I took turns pulling. If I'd known about the wagon, we probably would have made it to the wading creek. Then again, if we'd made it to wading, we might not have had prairie chicken and eggs, so it was a fair enough trade.

"I'm going to put up a notice at the general, and the restaurant. You can post your letters and put one up there."

I nodded, and patted the bundle I had tucked into my pocket. The bundle of letters home warmed me, something to take my mind off the new torment that was my old corset.

As much as I had wished for it back, I was glad that Birdie hadn't insisted on lacing it tight. Even let out, the corset's bones bit my skin. The calluses—mental or physical—that I'd once possessed had softened.

I still ached from wearing the thing the night before, and now its stricture irritated me doubly. I had the unenviable sense that I would be left wanting whether I wore it or not.

"And don't forget," Birdie continued, as if running down a mental list. "It's two dollars to have you come, period. They're paying for your appearance, not for the water."

My papa would have enjoyed that bit of wordplay, and I didn't argue. I could promise no one a running well or a good spring. I could only tell them what I saw, and it was best if that came with no positive guarantee.

Nevertheless, my heart beat an odd pattern, my nerves wearing with the unknown. I knew how easily a benign gift could turn malignant. Taking the wagon over for Birdie, I tried to put those thoughts aside as West Glory finally came into view.

With sunrise behind it, it was a darling little town. Morning light painted it in fresh hues of pink and gold. It even gilded the dust. So far, I liked mornings best of all in the Territories.

"Leave the cart here," Birdie said. She leaned down to wake Louella, making her unfold her jelly arms and legs to wrap around her. She nodded down the street. "The post office is down a ways. You'll pass the—"

Pleased with myself, I told her, "I know where it is. That's how I found your homestead."

"Good girl," Birdie said. She shifted Louella onto her hip. "When you're done, cross over to the restaurant and wait for me. I shouldn't take long at all."

The walk to the post office was short, but I admit, I dawdled. I looked through plate glass windows into a feed store, which seemed nothing more than a floor filled with overflowing barrels of grain.

Then I peeked into the barber's, which was a mistake. A man in a white coat was busy pulling out a tooth with tongs so barbaric that I thought I might have nightmares.

Hurrying along, I got a look into the saloon, though I smelled it first. Papa only occasionally indulged, but the thick, hoppy scent of beer wafting out made me homesick nonetheless. A woman scrubbed at the bar—hard labor to polish all that wood.

These slices of a different kind of life in the West teased my imagination. It was a bit more like what I'd expected, though hardly the anarchy that papers back home had described. And it was paler than I'd anticipated.

Baltimore was a rainbow of nationalities, a port to the world. Save the Indian woman I'd seen on the first day, West Glory was peopled with third-generation English and Irish alone.

You can always leave, I told myself.

I pushed open the post office door and marveled that I'd thought that at all. That I would spend the rest of my life in service here had been immutable to me just the month before. Was this progress? And if it was, was I happy with it?

If I had been, it ended the moment I took a breath. The air smelled of burnt black powder. The plastered walls bore dark pits, round as cherries, and I stared at them helplessly. In my mind alone, I saw a flash of fire, and blood. So much blood. An uncanny temperature, somehow hot and cold at once, gripped me.

"You all right, miss?"

The unfamiliar voice jerked me back from the past, and I was grateful for it. It belonged to a young man, who moved to hold the door for me so I could come the rest of the way in. His sun-bleached hair and bright eyes were kind, burning away the remnants of my dark memory.

"I'm fine, thank you," I murmured.

With a snort, the clerk broke in. "Quit sniffing at her, Royal. You can tell looking at her that she's too good for you. Now, as for me . . ."

Rolling his eyes, Royal stepped aside and gave me his place at the counter. "Pay him no mind," he told me; it was good advice. The clerk still wore his leer, and I did my best to avoid his gaze.

"I've got several to post," I told the counter, and pulled my bundle from my pocket. A letter for my friends back home to share, and several for Mama. Birdie said she hadn't wired home about my arrival by fire, so I'd written it in pages instead.

I'd done my best to make it sound like a merry diversion — how amusing to be there for a stagecoach robbery! — and the time I'd spent with Emerson directly thereafter was edited for propriety. In Mama's version of the story, he picked me up and took me straight to Aunt Birdie's.

The newspapers weren't the only ones who creatively shaped the story of the West for back-home readers.

"May I post a bill?" I asked, gesturing toward the wall.

The clerk handed me a nail from behind the counter. "Whatever makes you happy, girlie. Just pound that in with the rock."

And indeed, there was a rock sitting in the corner, just for nailing in posters, apparently. It was so absurd, I actually smiled. Taking it up, I skimmed the wall, trying to find a good place for mine. Not next to Emmett and Bob Dalton, wanted for murder and train robbery, for certain.

Bypassing the malcontents, I found the more ordinary notices—things for sale, services on offer. One stopped me, and I read a little tragedy in its terse presentation:

> **Healthy young mother of four, one deceased, having an excess of milk will wet-nurse a child in her own home.**

Quelling my jumbled emotions, I pounded my notice in beneath that one. Replacing the rock, I went to leave, and the young man opened the door for me again.

"You have a real good day," he said.

I know I thanked him—my mother had taught me well

enough — but I had no recollection of it. For it was when he spoke again that I knew his voice and his blue eyes. He had robbed me and left me to the elements in the empty prairie. Surely he recognized me.

I could only pray he didn't know *I* had recognized *him*.

Nine

"There she is," Birdie said when I pushed into the foyer of the restaurant. She sat at the end of a long table, tying a napkin around Louella's neck.

With wallpaper behind her and good china before her, I saw clearly the Beatrice Stewart who'd charmed Baltimore entirely and let Peter Neal steal her off to Kansas. Petty and Birdie, full of hope and joy—with no idea how soon they'd be parted.

I hurried to sit next to her, glad to put my back to the windows. I didn't want to look through them and accidentally catch another glimpse of Royal. And likewise, I didn't care for him to catch sight of me with my family. Birdie hefted a shotgun with ease and confidence, it was true, but I preferred to avoid the need entirely.

"I thought we'd have a treat," Birdie said. She poured Louella a glass of milk from the pitcher between us, then offered it to me. "I know you've been missing your mama's cooking. Mrs. Herrington's not quite the genius in the kitchen Pauline is, but she makes a fine powder biscuit."

Though I greedily poured a glass of milk for myself, I asked, "Do you think we should? We've still got a bit of stew left over, and I know where to find more wild eggs . . ."

"The way I see it — " Birdie said. She smiled when a raw-boned woman shuffled toward the table, put down several covered dishes, then returned to the kitchen. Birdie continued, "It's just ten engagements for you, to buy a cow. We can afford a dollar for breakfast."

That expectation bore down on me. Smoothing my napkin in my lap, I said, "I hope I get that many, then."

"I like a biscuit," Louella said to no one in particular.

Birdie started uncovering the serving dishes. Watching her, I realized she was just this side of *giddy*. My newfound gift was some kind of salvation for her; it put stars in her eyes and warmth in her smile. All her cheer made my unease seem selfish — it's not as though she planned to mine me for diamonds and pearls.

"Between here and Jubilee, we'll find plenty of takers."

"What's that about Jubilee?" a thin, whey-faced man at the next table asked. It startled me, honestly, that he would interrupt a conversation just because he could over-hear it.

Birdie turned to him. "You mind your business, Carl, and I'll mind mine."

Though Carl huffed into his coffee, he didn't seem perturbed at Birdie's remonstration. In fact, he took a sip from his cup and tipped his chair back on two legs to better insert himself into our party.

"I'm just saying, whatever this missy's got on offer, I expect we have enough decent people in West Glory to keep her busy without resorting to mixing with—"

"The war's been over twenty-five years, sir, and you lost. Now, if you wouldn't mind terribly, I'm trying to have breakfast." Then, with a smile as sweet as honey, Birdie put a finger on his chair and tipped it back on all four legs.

I buried my laughter in my napkin. Though she was blond and lithe where Mama was brunette and broad, I could see very much the family resemblance in that moment.

Still, Carl leaned toward me and offered me his card. "If it's cooking, cleaning, or washing, you look me up, sweetheart. I'll keep you working right here at home."

"I shall keep your kind offer in mind," I told him, and turned back to my plate without taking his card. No young lady was obligated to receive a card; refusing it was the only insult I could give him and keep my manners intact.

"Oh!" Birdie hopped up suddenly. "Stay here and mind Lou, Zora. I'll be right back."

She flitted away in haste, and I twisted round to follow her. My stays dug viciously, reminding me that well-mannered girls didn't gawk. I lost track of her, but her abrupt exit explained itself soon enough.

When she came back inside, she came on Theo's elbow. He wore yet another suit this morning, or, at least, most of one. Black trousers beneath a patterned mulberry waistcoat and black tie — there was surely a matching jacket hanging by his bed. Everything he wore was fitted, so he cut a re-fined figure, indeed.

"Look who I found," Birdie said, all but shoving Theo toward the empty seat at my left. "Do sit and have breakfast with us, won't you?"

I felt sorry for him, at the mercy of my merciless aunt, and so I offered a smile and a nod. "Please do."

Not to be left out, Louella added, "Do!"

That made Theo laugh, and he relaxed, slipping into the seat next to me. "I'm honored to enjoy such lovely company, thank you."

"I was just telling Mr. de la Croix that we were headed to Jubilee — "

Carl, behind us, snorted. Birdie replied with a well-placed elbow to the back of his chair, then continued her thought gracefully. "And he was kind enough to offer us a ride in his buggy. Isn't that good of him, Louella?"

Narrowing my eyes at my sneaky aunt, I let Louella answer the question instead of indulging her. Of course, Louella was happy to oblige, since she had already once been denied the novelty of a buggy ride.

"I'm still breaking it in," Theo told me as he reached for a biscuit. "So really, it's a favor to me."

I forgot myself, and joked, "Any excuse will do, is that it?"

Frowning slightly, he said, "Pardon?"

Immediately, with apologies, I withdrew the jest. It had been rude to offer it at all, but I couldn't help but think that Theo would fare poorly with my cousins at home.

That, and if offered the same insult, I truly believed Emerson Birch would have only laughed.

～～～～～

Though Birdie and I had previously enjoyed the pleasure, Louella was fantastically impressed with Theo's buggy. Birdie climbed in first so Theo could deliver Louella directly into her arms. Even with the step, my little cousin was far too tiny to climb up.

"Miss Stewart," Theo said, when it came to my turn.

His gloves lay on the seat, and mine had been lost, so his bare hand smoothed over mine. Unmarred and silken, it reminded me that my Thomas' hands had been nothing of the kind. And, it was awful to acknowledge, neither were Emerson's.

Hitching my skirt, I climbed into the buggy, ignoring how directly he considered me. I didn't feel precious in his gaze; I felt guilty. As though I should be delighted that he'd noticed me at all—but did I deliberately douse a fire that was lit? I didn't; Theo was sincere enough, gentle enough—generous enough. But he was no tinder at all.

Birdie had developed a kind of telepathy, because the moment I settled next to her, she leaned in to whisper into my ear. "He's come a long way to make amends, Zora. Enough with your suffering; make the best of the bed you made."

Slapped without a touch, I corrected my posture until I sat perfect as a mannequin and no more animated.

The buggy barely shifted when Theo climbed in. As he took up the reins, he smiled and asked, "Onward, ladies?"

"Please," I replied.

"Won't this be fun?" Birdie asked Lou, clapping the

baby's hands together in delight. Then she cut me a pointed look. "Don't you think, Zora?"

"Oh yes. I do like this phaeton," I said finally. "We had an old victoria at home that my mother thought was a racing model, but you can fairly fly in this."

He laughed, shaking his head. "It makes me nervous, I admit. I'm used to driving on cobble and pavement."

"But you can barely feel the ruts and bumps," Birdie said. Though she sat between us, her interjection seemed an intrusion. For someone who had so deliberately ordered me to open myself to Theo, she was hardly acting the silent, sentinel chaperone. In fact, she went on. "And what is your horse's name?"

Before he could reply, I said, "Annabel Lee, of course."

"Do you like Mr. Poe, then?" Birdie asked.

"I do. I know many consider his poetry mawkish and morbid, but I rather like the depth of it."

Birdie tangled her fingers with Louella's, playing a weaving game with their hands to keep her entertained. "I prefer Blake, myself. I like a bit of joy in my reading."

"You're both mad." I shrugged lazily, brushing a loose curl from my face. "If you're going to indulge in poetry, it should transport you at the least. 'Goblin Market,' now, that's a poem."

Considering this, Theo pursed his lips. Then suddenly, he recited, his honey voice flowing smooth, barely stolen by the wind. *"Figs to fill your mouth, citrons from the South, sweet to tongue and sound to eye; come buy, come buy."*

He'd surprised me; I could admit that. I skipped a few lines and answered, *" 'Lie close,' Laura said, pricking up her golden head: 'We must not look at goblin men.' "*

"There's a child present," Birdie said. She smoothed her hands over Louella's ears, as if a scrap of verse could slip in and poison her tender thoughts. Then she cleared her throat and changed the subject. "Have you had any news, Mr. de la Croix?"

Taking his correction far better than I, Theo kept his merry face and didn't hesitate in his reply. With a gentle hand, he urged Annabel Lee a bit faster now that we had come to open prairie, and replied, "Are you acquainted with Mr. and Mrs. Bader? They're having a barn raising this Saturday, all invited."

Birdie clapped Louella's hands together, making a happy sound. "Will you be there?"

"I thought I might. I could stand learning to use a hammer and nail," Theo said. His gaze trailed toward me again. "And I understand there's a dance afterwards."

"Is there?" I said, committing myself to nothing.

"There always is," Birdie said, delight coursing through her. She actually bounced a bit, disguised as dandling Louella on her knees playfully. "Pretty girls and handsome boys dancing into the night. Won't that be gay?"

Because I was behaving, I simply agreed.

Ten

Unlike West Glory, Jubilee had a sign at the town limits. It was decorated with hand-carved scrollwork, and someone had taken care to fill the words in with gold paint:

JUBILEE
Our Chariot Carried Us Home
All Free Men Welcome

The sentiment warmed me, and as Theo parked his phaeton in front of the general store, I looked around to discover the sign was rather more than sentiment. As peach and pale as West Glory was, Jubilee was every shade of brown and russet.

It was, in all ways imaginable, a western town, exact in

content to West Glory, down to the post office. It was simply that everyone I saw was black—the two dusty cowboys who tipped their hats at us as they rode past, the shopkeepers peering from windows, a little girl in pink calico chasing a hoop with a stick.

It was as if someone had split Baltimore's rainbow and I had finally found both halves.

Theo let the step down, and I clambered from the buggy, followed in quick succession by my aunt and cousin. Birdie fished through her pockets, handing me another notice to post. "Come inside, duck, I need to talk to Mrs. Franklin."

Louella pointed to the girl with the hoop. "Play?"

"You may *ask* to play," Birdie told her, brushing the dust from Louella's skirts. "When you're done, you come right back."

With a nod, Louella bounded off, and Theo moved to open the door for us. He didn't follow us, though. When Birdie looked back to him, he said, "I'm just going to stretch my legs a bit."

The general was warm inside, and a little dark. But it smelled like heaven, of anise and cinnamon and cocoa. I inhaled deeply, then sighed aloud in pleasure. A trembling passed beneath my feet, and I clapped a hand over my mouth to keep in a laugh. I had been gone so long from civilization that the wealth in a general had undone me.

The woman at the counter—Mrs. Franklin, I imagined—shook her head at me, seemingly both curious and amused. Brushing past me, Birdie went directly to the counter, explaining me in an offhand way, "That's the niece I was telling you about."

"Pretty girl," Mrs. Franklin said.

"Exactly," was Birdie's reply.

Whatever conversation they were continuing about me, I wasn't entirely sure I wanted to hear the rest of it. So I scuttled away to explore the bounties the general had on offer. My pockets were entirely empty, but dreaming was free.

Fifty-gallon barrels stood in neat lines, the lids open to present their riches. Dry beans and peas, flour and cornmeal—then, nearby, nails and laundry pins and one barrel piled tantalizingly high with white soap flakes.

I picked one of the laundry pins up, rubbing its smooth head thoughtfully. If only we had a tree or a post at Birdie's—hanging the wash to dry would speed that chore by hours.

But as we had no trees, and line was expensive, I returned the pin to its barrel and regretfully moved on. Sniffing at a box of black and orange tea, I shivered at the richness. Then I raised a box of coffee beans, enjoying the way they whispered when jostled.

As I replaced the coffee, a man's voice caught my attention. "Let's take a look at what you've got, Birch."

With a tentative step toward it, I did my best to disguise spying as window shopping. Though I had no need of pipe tobacco, I nonetheless went to study the many varieties available. Through a swinging door in the back, I saw Emerson's wavy, sun-streaked hair.

"This one's irregular," Emerson said. Through the door's slats, I caught small glimpses of his trade—an impressive collection of pelts, in shades of gray and brown, spilling out like silk. "But the rest are good."

Returning the tobacco to the shelf, I walked ever so casually toward the feed bins. From that angle, I saw both Emerson and, I assumed, Mr. Franklin. It only made sense. He wore a city-cut suit, and Husband and Wife Herrington ran the general in West Glory. But the more I thought on it, the more I hesitated. This man seemed rather older than Mrs. Franklin—his black curls were streaked with silver. Perhaps he was a father-in-law?

And as I stood there making up stories and family trees, guessing at who might be related to whom, the door separating me from the back room glided open as if by magic.

"I thought," Emerson said, tipping his head slightly to meet my gaze, "that you could eavesdrop more readily if it were open."

Since he wanted to make me blush, I refused. I walked right in as if I belonged there, and with much cheek, I said,

"Thank you, Mr. Birch." Turning, I offered my hand. "Pleasure to meet you, Mr. —"

"Gibson," he said, shaking my hand.

"This is Miss Stewart," Emerson said. "She's counting her days until she can go back home to Baltimore."

"Mr. Birch is given to fantasy, as I'm sure you know."

Mr. Gibson laughed. "I'm too smart to get caught up in your affairs, children." He piled the pelts in a basket, then told Emerson, "Let me go tot these up; I'll give Sal your credit slip."

"Much obliged," Emerson said, holding the door open for him as well. When it swung closed, it brought a draft of the perfumed air from the front of the store.

I hadn't realized how starved I was for novelty until that moment, when I drew another long breath to savor the scents. Puffed up with luxury, I suddenly realized that I stood there alone—with Emerson. Composing myself, I said, "How is your well?"

"Fine as your garden, I expect."

"My aunt thinks it finally caught up with the season."

He raised an eyebrow, because it *was* ridiculous to think that an entire plot could come to its senses overnight and start to bloom. But he put no words to the truth and instead said, "And what finds you in Jubilee?"

"My aunt's trying to hire me out as a—a springsweet."

His word felt silver and slick on my tongue, a connection that hummed like a harp string. I could in no way be sure that he felt it, and yet I was certain he did. It shone in his eyes, swirling there among the green and the amber and blue.

Then it ebbed away and he said, "Probably good money in that."

"I hope so." Though I owed no explanation, I gave one anyway. "We'd like to buy a cow before winter."

Emerson nodded, curling and uncurling his fingers on the top of the swinging door. It seemed he weighed a thought, measuring it before deciding finally to share. "Folks'll turn on you quicker than you think."

Stilled by hesitation, I nodded. I remembered well how glad strangers were to have their futures from Amelia, as long as their futures pleased them. When that pleasure turned, it had become vicious. Rubbing my hands together, I admitted, "It's dire, or I wouldn't consider it."

Emerson glanced past me, then skimmed his fingers down my arm. "Be careful."

His whisper was almost as intimate as his touch. Softly, I reassured him, "I will be. I'm promising them nothing."

"That's what *you* think." He pushed the door open, then added, "And that's not dramatics, Miss Stewart. Hope's hard to come by out here. If you go around telling people you can find water, and they don't have any to find . . ."

My throat closed. Because this time, Emerson wasn't barbing me or begging for a retort. He warned me in earnest, and I had a feeling he had some kind of experience to inform it. Sadly, so did I.

"I'll be careful," I said.

Nudging me out of the back room, the temper between us changed. He said, almost conversationally, "Did you know there's a creek round about two miles from your back door?"

That question prickled on my skin, a sheen of awareness rising to the surface. Had he seen the silver gleaming I made, when he dug into our garden? Had he memorized my ghost map of the plains, the one outlined with elemental magic?

Rather than ask, I answered. "As a matter of fact, I did."

"There's a stand of trees nearby," he said. "Sometimes I like to rest Epona there, on the way back from Enid Station. There's sand plums out that way, if you know where to look."

Though he drifted away from me, our eyes still met. "Our hens aren't laying yet, so I've been stealing eggs from the prairie chickens near there. Do you often go to Enid?"

"Often enough. I might tomorrow, to see what the 3:15 train brings in."

The harp string sang again—it was an invitation.

I selected a box of sassafras filé from the shelves to sample. The vibrant spice burned pleasantly, but not as much as the tilt of Emerson's brows when I nodded.

He'd asked and I'd accepted, come what may.

~~~~~~

"This should be it," Birdie said, consulting a scrap of paper, then shielding her eyes to look into the distance. Louella dozed in her lap, and Birdie stroked her curls smooth with a steady touch.

A weathered wooden stake marked this plot as 443. Mr. Gibson had said its owners might receive us. Nothing stood near the stake, however, and considering that each citizen who'd claimed land in last year's run had taken 160 acres, the front edge may have been the farthest point from the house.

Theo slowed Annabel Lee and pointed to a dark spot in the field. "Perhaps there?"

Considering the distance and the babe in her lap, Birdie weighed her options. Finally, she turned to Theo. "Would you mind if I stayed here? She's so peaceful."

"Not at all," Theo said. He twisted the reins in the foot-board rail. Then he stood and hefted the canopy, unfolding it to cast a deep shade over Birdie and Louella. "How's that?"

Birdie graced him with a smile. "Lovely, thank you." She

handed me the introductory note Mr. Gibson had written. "Unless you've got a flair for showmanship, keep to the letter."

Though I wanted to, I didn't roll my eyes at her. Tucking the introduction into my pocket, I let Theo help me from the carriage but declined his arm as we started toward the dark spot.

"I need both hands if I fall," I told him. "I'm clumsy."

Rumbling with amusement, he slipped his hands into his pockets and strode along with me smoothly. "Of this, I am aware, Miss Stewart. You were sure-footed as could be on that fountain until suddenly you were not."

"That's one way to put it," I conceded.

Theo tipped his head back, catching the slanting afternoon sun on his face. He looked rather like a Persian prince, bronzed by the sunlight, his dark hair trying to escape its ribbon. "Then you disappeared entirely; I was agog."

Thinking on it, I could summon the sensation of the cold, the marrow-deep ache of the water as it swallowed me. But it seemed awfully long ago, the dazzling peace I'd felt beneath the surface only slightly recalled.

I told him, "It was deep as a well."

"I know," he replied. "I went in after you."

The grass all around us whispered, stirred by a warm breeze. Trailing my hand across the shifting surface, I plucked a sprig of wild indigo. A ladder of pale blue flowers clung to the stem, and I broke it in half. I slipped a bit behind my ear, then offered the rest to Theo for his buttonhole. "I never did thank you for that."

"And you mustn't. I don't believe in it, gratitude for things that should be a given." Then, as an afterthought, he added with much fire, "I would have gone in after anyone; it wasn't particular to you."

Patting his shoulder, I reassured him, "You're every inch the gentleman."

Theo relaxed a bit, washed over with vindication. "I believe in chivalry."

"Oh, I don't," I replied. "A knight always gets to have his cake and eat it too, doesn't he? 'Hello, my lady, I love you—but I must run off to find the Holy Grail now. Wait for me!'"

Cross, Theo considered me from the corner of his eye. "That's not chivalry at all. And finding the Grail would be an honorable quest."

"Says the man who would get to ride after it and savor all sorts of adventure in the search." I shrugged; I had hardly designed the way of the world. I was simply subject to it. "I assure you, there are absolutely no epic ways to make a sampler or to roast a lamb shank."

"So you're a suffragette," Theo declared.

I stopped and turned to him. "What if I am?"

And amazingly, Theo quailed. He honestly lost a shade of color from his handsome face, and his brows tented ever so slightly in horror, as if I had pulled open my coat to reveal a clockwork heart, or perhaps a second head growing just beneath my breast. It lasted just a minute, but the impression lingered, even as he recovered. "I don't see why women shouldn't have the vote."

"That's very generous of you," I said. Then I reached out to straighten his sprig of indigo. "But I don't believe we were talking about the vote."

He stood there quietly, perhaps wondering how the conversation had veered so wildly from his expectations. Eyes too dark to read, he pulled his shoulders back and straightened his posture. The wind tossed a stray lock of his hair; he cut quite a regal figure against the darkening sky.

But then, as if he had brushed aside some minor inconvenience, he said, "It *was* a house, it seems. There's someone in the yard."

What a pity he could neither draw nor concede. All his effort to follow me, from burying ground to ball to the great open plains, had been an effort to satisfy his curiosity and none of mine at all. I was the thing *he* wanted, but his affection was an unwanted calling card. I was in no way obligated to accept.

"So there is," I said agreeably, and I stepped past him to introduce myself.

~~~~~~~~~~

"We've dug two wells now," Mr. Cole said, pointing them out. "The first one did nothing but seep. Ivetta caught more water in her teacups than we got out of that thing."

Ivetta watched us from the front of the house, an infant curled on her shoulder. Something about her coal-dark eyes and gaunt cheeks haunted me; she didn't cough, or sweat with a fever, but it was plain she wasn't well. Her wrists were leather-clad bones, much like the knuckle she offered the baby to suck.

Mr. Cole interrupted my thoughts, pointing out the second well. This one had a lid, which Theo held so Mr. Cole could draw the bucket up. "And this one, well, you see it. Half water, half mud. Gotta strain it through cheesecloth and boil it to get a sip."

"That's terrible," I said, peering into the bucket.

Letting the bucket back down, Mr. Cole sighed. "The government says we have to make a living here five years before the land's ours to keep. The way it's going, we're hardly going to make it two. We're hurting, Miss Stewart."

The way he laid it out, so plain, without embellishment, it felt like a tattooing in my flesh. From this very first introduction, I couldn't mistake this as playing. These were no amusing social calls; there would be no cakes and laughter. Everything I said would be of consequence; Emerson's warning came back to me and set my heart to trembling.

"Let me see what I can do," I said.

For my own ease, I walked away from them, trailing into the field to give myself a center of quiet. First my breath, then my will, I reached inside to find the pulse within me that matched the pulse without, thrumming through the earth to sustain it.

I wanted it so badly; I ached to give the Coles good news, to be the one to deliver fresh water and three more years on their land. The wind picked up, and blessedly, I tasted water on it. Turning slowly, seeking the sweetest point of it, I opened my eyes and gazed in wonder.

The silver trace of water ran all around us; I could see the paltry stream feeding the current well. Following it, drawing breath in the same weight and time, I sought its source. Though I had no sense of depth, I plainly saw a bright well before me, and I walked toward it.

When I stood on top of it, in the glimmering threads of my vision, it was just as if I had plunged into the fountain again. I ached with cold clarity. It clasped me and caressed me, pulling through my hair, swirling across my skin. I honestly felt that if I only tried, I could call it up.

But that was madness, just an artifact of seeing the impossible. Pressing a hand to my heart to calm it, I called out. "I beg you dig here, sir."

When Mr. Cole and Theo took spades to dry earth, at first I feared that I had called them on a useless errand. The ground yielded nothing; soon, they both stood knee-deep in the excavation, and nothing came.

Petty terror ran on my skin; I begged the water to come. I clutched my hands together and prayed in earnest. When I closed my eyes, I saw the sad, dark hollow of Ivetta's face and that poor babe wanting more than a dry knuckle to soothe it.

I looked into the silvered map again. Burying my nails in my hands, I pulled from some inward place. I strained toward the firmament, denying the loam its vicious hold—it was almost a song in me, a call from the water in my flesh to the water in the earth, to unite.

Perhaps overcome with my effort, I thought—for a singular moment—that the earth moved beneath my feet. That something had split deep below, that I might have drawn the water up by sheer force and inexplicable magic.

Quite calmly, Mr. Cole said, "You better hop out, son."

My eyes burned, stupid tears promising to spill over, salt water no one could use. Except then I saw Theo throw his spade and Mr. Cole's after it. He scrambled up, hauling Mr. Cole out just as a geyser erupted.

A singular, spectacular spray arced against the sky. It threw crystalline beads like loose pearls; they rained on my shoulders and cooled my face. Then, as gloriously as it rose, it receded. The well filled to the surface and overflowed; water swirled and lapped at the heaps of earth displaced in the digging.

And Mr. Cole, a mature gentleman by my standard, knelt in the new mud and cried.

Eleven

That evening, I stood over a pot of boiling bones, steam like sweat on my face as Birdie sorted through her sewing box for worn patterns.

As the Coles hadn't expected us, we hadn't expected payment. All I asked was that they seed the community with the good news, and I was certain they would. But they also insisted on giving me a fox skin.

It was smooth and well-tanned, probably worth a great deal more than the two dollars that was my asking price. Since we were unlikely to get another, Birdie decided it would make a good pair of gloves for Louella.

"I wanted to tell you something," I said, brushing my face dry before going back to my stirring.

"Tell away, duck," Birdie replied.

I tapped the spoon on the side of the pot to disguise some of my words from Louella's ears. "The men who robbed me . . . I saw one of them in town today."

Birdie took a pin from between her lips. "Royal Wakes, I imagine. Ellis keeps himself scarce."

"You know?" I all but dropped the spoon in surprise. It had been such an ugly secret coiled in my chest, one I had borne through our trip to Jubilee and our stop at the Coles'. I hadn't wanted to bring Theo into it or speak it so directly that Louella would pay attention and understand. But now that it was out, with so insignificant a reaction, I could barely contain myself.

Turning the fox skin to measure it, Birdie glanced over her shoulder at me. "Everyone does, Zora. But it's best we keep the Wakes brothers. They never harm anyone."

"I could have been —"

"But you weren't." She turned back to her sewing. "Sometimes you put up with the bad to avoid the worse. The Dalton boys haven't got a soul to share between them. At least Royal walks around looking like he feels guilty."

I didn't know what to say. Perhaps I had a great deal more to learn about living in the West, but what was the purpose in having a sheriff and a marshal, and a jail right in town, if they were nothing but decoration? I couldn't believe how casually Birdie took it and how easily she said, "Promise me you'll keep it to yourself."

Betrayed, I could only shake my head. But her betrayal made it that much easier to lie to her. "In any case . . . I think tomorrow," I said, attempting to disguise my plotting as casual conversation, "I shall go back to those nests and see if I can't find more eggs."

Birdie hummed her agreement, raising a pattern to check it for defect. Lamplight shone through the worn tissue paper, casting a dreamy glow on Birdie's face. "That will be a treat. I wouldn't complain if you brought another chicken."

"I can't imagine I will."

"Zora!" Louella exclaimed. She swung a little fist and laughed, settling in with her grass dolls. "Zora hit the birdie!"

"Yes, I did, and surprised us both." I laughed to myself, for that seemed to be the most excitement Louella had ever enjoyed. Then, thoughtfully, I said, "I should write to Papa and have him send instructions for string traps. He made them when he was a boy; he used to brag about them."

Birdie smoothed a pattern out, then plucked a pin from her sewing box. "Shame we only have the one shotgun."

"Isn't it?" I said, and didn't mean it at all.

Let her believe I'd kit myself out like Annie Oakley and go hunting. Since it was fantasy, it harmed nothing and kept me from having to refuse it. A sharpness pricked at my heart, and I drained from it: I had tucked Thomas' dance card in my corset and put them both away.

Now it seemed to accuse—how many hours had passed since I'd considered him? Certainly I'd given him no thought at all when I agreed to meet Emerson at the creek, when I lied to my aunt to make that meeting possible.

"Do you think about Petty?" I asked softly.

Then Birdie and I both looked to Louella. I should have measured the question before I asked it, but the baby was happily distracted with her grass doll. Birdie moved a bit closer to answer.

"It's hard not to." Gesturing faintly at the soddy, she said, "This was his dream. Wide-open spaces, answering to no man . . ."

Fishing the bones from the soup, I put them aside to be cracked for marrow. "Didn't you have that in Kansas?"

Birdie made a faraway sound that might have been laughter once. "It got too crowded, he said. We could see our neighbors from our porch. We had a porch then, and glass for our windows. A wagon and a pony . . ."

I didn't have to ask what happened to them. Everything was dear in the Territories—no doubt they sold them all, to start again on this prairie. How cruel for the first winter to fell him.

"Why don't you go home? You know Mama would love to have you and Louella to fuss over."

Birdie squinted at me. "I *am* home."

Quickly, I apologized. She said it as if I should have realized that; simple Zora, somehow failing to understand something so integral to her being. Heat stung my cheeks, and I stammered to recover. "I didn't mean anything by it."

"Of course not." Birdie clasped the back of my neck, giving me a shake. She was so very like my mother in that moment; I wondered if I were like them, too. Rubbing her thumb against the nape of my neck, Birdie said, "Don't take this personally, duck. You're young and foolish and running away. That doesn't mean we all are."

I did take it personally. Bristling like a boar, I was quite short when I replied, "I came here deliberately. If it hadn't been your home, it would have been a widower's."

"If the destination didn't matter," Birdie said, taking the spoon from my hand, "then how is that anything *but* running away?"

She struck me silent a moment. When I finally rose to my own defense, it was with a change of subject. Stiffly, I said, "My indiscretion at the ball was incidental, I hope you're aware."

"Oh, I'm aware." Tasting the broth, Birdie made a face. "Pauline writes exceptionally detailed letters. I think she's a frustrated novelist."

"A means to an end. Ruination in Baltimore meant I could choose my path thereafter." I lifted my chin. "My plans are honorable; Thomas meant to spend his life caring for people, so that's what I'll do in his stead."

"You can't live his life." And that simply, Birdie clasped my face in her hands. They were worn rough, hard living taking a hard toll on fingertips that were once, no doubt, as smooth as my mama's. "You can only live yours."

It was a thoughtful sentiment. A good one. But before I could appreciate it, Birdie continued.

"And you, ducky, made a promise with a kiss that Mr. de la Croix was good enough to come all this way to help you keep."

Pulling away, I decided it would be an excellent time to draw some water. As I pulled a bonnet over my head, I cast petty words in my wake. "You're fascinated by his many merits. Why don't *you* marry him?"

"Bachelors don't marry widows," Birdie said, and worst of it—worst!—was that she smiled at me! The same indulgent expression she saved for Louella's mad follies—she thought me silly and childish!

The tragedy of a soddy was that the door was fixed

tight—one can neither throw it open in a fury nor slam it shut in the same. This did not, however, prevent me from trying it. And infuriatingly, when I failed at both and stalked outside all the same, I heard Birdie call after me.

"Enjoy your run, Zora!"

~~~~~~~~

I didn't run. The yoke was too heavy, and I still wore my heeled town shoes. By the time I reached the well, I hurt inside and out. The blister I'd developed on my ankle would be a curse, stupid penance for stupid temper.

Dropping the hateful yoke by the well cover, I sank down beside it. The ground was no tender bed, but the sky was an extraordinary quilt—stars bright as match sparks, the Milky Way a delicate lace that banded the heavens.

I knew their many patterns, the ancient stories written into the night—but what good did it do me, to know why Berenice's Hair was there? Would it ever matter that I could find the Crow, the Serpent Bearer? I'd made a grave mistake of tactics at the Sugarcane Ball, and now, it seemed, all that mattered was rectifying it.

Though I lay there alone, I argued with Birdie nonetheless. I hadn't run from anything!

There was nothing left for me in Baltimore but a cold stone. I didn't care to dance or gossip anymore. I had no taste for tea and cookies and conversation about Miss Bly's clever circumnavigation of the world. I felt nothing there but a hollowness.

Didn't it make good sense to make myself useful?

The wind carried a song to me, and for a moment, I thought I had imagined it. But the tuneful notes were entirely unfamiliar, drumming low like the pulse I felt when I reached for the water beneath. Stirring from my rest, I sharpened my attention.

The song drew me to my feet, and I turned as if wound with a key. The darkness of the prairie without a moon was uniform and almost complete. Nothing made shadows, for all was in shadow, inky blue and velvet.

But then, as I pressed a hand to my brow, I caught sight of motion. Silhouettes. Some went on horses, and some on foot. I could see nothing but their shapes on the horizon; I heard only the sweet lullaby that marked their progress.

The childish part of me wondered if they might be fairies, parading in Avalon and visible only because I had lain in the dew beneath the new moon.

Or perhaps they were a ghostly burial procession, which Buffalo Bill's articles had often invoked. I was too far west for it to be Mr. Lincoln's spectral train, but the possibility chilled me nonetheless.

Gathering the yoke and buckets, I backed toward the soddy. The wind changed, and the music drifted away. The notes reverberated within me, but the night seemed strangely alive. Tall grasses caught my wrists; the sullen night birds called out my name.

Then a golden thread of light streaked toward me, and I turned to see Aunt Birdie at the edge of the garden. She held the tin lantern aloft in one hand and her shotgun in the other. Softly, she said, "Zora?"

I hurried to her side and put a hand on her shoulder to reassure her. "Here I am."

"Do you hear that?" she asked, her voice still low.

And I nodded, for when the wind shifted once more, it brought back the unfamiliar song. But because Birdie whispered, so did I. Pointing toward the horizon, I said, "I saw them, just over there. Do you think it's a haunting?"

"No, I think it's the Arapaho."

I peered into the dark, as if I might see the travelers better now that I knew I looked for men and women instead of shades and fairies. But it seemed they had already passed beyond my sight. If I closed my eyes, I could hear their song, but I couldn't swear that it wasn't my own imagination.

Handing me the lantern, Birdie tried to hide the furrow of her brow, smoothing it with her fingertips. But her unease was evident, drawing her voice and her breath taut. "Don't you mention this when you go calling."

Baffled, I asked, "Why?"

"To keep the peace with our neighbors. Petty agreed to wire off our plot, but he never did." Birdie nudged me into the house, casting a look over her shoulder. "We never intended to; didn't see the harm in letting people come and go."

I watched as she put the bolt in the door then hung the shotgun above it. "But you do now?"

"No, ma'am," Birdie said, and turned to me. "But we're three women out here alone. I'd rather not give the town fools and Indian haters something to stew about if we can help it."

Leaning into her, all I could say was "Oh."

Birdie seemed very like a shade of herself as she took the seat by the stove, reaching for the marrow bones to pick clean.

She spared me no other glance, but murmured, "Go on to bed, Zora. It's been a long day."

I did lie down beside Louella, and I closed my eyes in truth. But after that, no sleep would come.

The morning came quiet and passed without incident. Though sometimes it seemed all chaos, life on Birdie's homestead had developed a kind of rhythm to it. Water, then breakfast, then chores. Water, then lunch, then chores. Water, then nap for Louella, and that's when I made my escape.

"I'll hurry," I told Birdie, tying on her apron.

And that wasn't a lie—once I was out of sight of the soddy, I all but ran. Two miles wouldn't take so long without a babe in tow, but it was still a ways, and I was unsure of the time. I had no watch, and I wished belatedly that I'd paid better attention to Miss Burnside's lessons on the Greeks. Surely, our newly tall cornstalks would make for brilliant sundials, if only I knew how to interpret their shadows.

Prairie chickens lowed when I hurried through their territory, and my heart picked up. Blessedly, nothing flew at me—I suspected that my singular luck the first time could not be repeated, and I didn't care to be pecked to death. The sun beat down, through my bonnet, through the thin cotton on my shoulders. But it was a pleasant heat, sweetened by green grass and the pungent tease of wild garlic in the air. And then I scented not water but earth. The rich, sweet scent of it newly turned over.

The gold and green of the prairie gave way to lush green.

It was like someone had touched a finger to the plains and drawn a meandering line, painting it with brighter colors than the rest of the world. Cattails rose up, their heads still smooth and immature but bowing toward the water that fed them.

My mouth stung with anticipation, a heady sensation of appetite that had nothing at all to do with knives and spoons. Parting the bladed grasses, I revealed the banks of the creek.

Frogs peeped sweetly, and I ducked when a dragonfly streaked past. It was big as a hummingbird, I thought, rather larger than his delicate, blue-winged cousins that visited Mama's garden.

Following the bank, I savored each step, each breath. After filling myself with the dry, roasted land for so long, drinking in water-washed air made me giddy. I wanted to pull off my shoes and go splashing; I wanted to lie in the shallows and let the current comb my hair.

The creek widened at a bend, and I stopped short. Epona grazed nearby, barely lifting her head to consider me. Nearby, the remains of a simple lunch warmed in the sun—a half-eaten apple, a crust of bread.

And there, on a bed of flattened reeds, Emerson napped in the sunlight. He'd covered his face with his battered hat and tucked his arms behind his head as a pillow.

He was a scandalous vision. His toes twitched as he dreamt. He'd rolled his sleeves up and unbuttoned his shirt a bit, baring bronzed skin. His suspenders, pulled off his shoulders, pooled at his waist. It was like I'd stumbled into his bedroom before he'd dressed.

And I had slept in his bed, wrapped in rough linens that smelled of his skin—it was too vivid to bear. Unrefined desires stirred in me, raw, luscious wanting that led somewhere I didn't entirely grasp.

Leaning down, I dipped my fingers in the creek and flicked water at his feet.

"I heard you coming," Emerson said from beneath his hat.

I laughed, a sudden sound that startled me; I was silly and ridiculous. "But you decided to greet me half-naked all the same. Your manners are atrocious, Mr. Birch."

"So I hear. Mostly from you."

Rising on his elbows, Emerson pushed his hat back to bare his face. And something about it moved me so—perhaps how soft he looked, just out of sleep.

How dark his lashes were. His smooth brow and strong jaw complemented the pretty delicacy of his mouth, and I was . . . staring at that mouth.

I looked away, as if I had to break the connection before I could look at him again in a more seemly way. And I came over to sit near him, but not too near. Recovered, I hoped, I said, "Then you must perversely enjoy my correction, or why would you be here?"

Emerson studied my face, his own half-smile growing. "Guess I hate thinking about you wandering around with nobody to snip at."

"So you admit you think about me," I teased.

But he caught me in a trap of my own devising. Reaching out, he curled a knuckle and smoothed it down my arm, and wavered not at all when he replied, "More than I meant to."

Twelve

A shock of infatuation caught me by surprise.

At least, I wanted it to be a surprise; I wished I could claim innocence. But in truth, I was a liar—and my own dupe. I hadn't found myself here by accident; I was no naïf led astray by wolfish intentions I didn't understand.

I chose it. I walked here with head up and eyes forward. And now, admitting that, I both ached and rebelled. *What would Thomas think?* I wondered, and then I realized—he would think nothing at all. If he could, I'd be in Annapolis, a newlywed, a doctor's wife.

Instead, I sat in new, green grass and reached up to catch Emerson's hand. Hooking my fingers around his, I said, "Aren't you forward?" But it came out wrong; my voice faint like powder and unlike myself entirely.

Emerson frowned, sitting up the rest of the way. "What's the matter?"

"Don't read my mind," I joked weakly, trying to soothe myself to composure. "It's rude, and you already have any number of marks against you."

Then, proving he couldn't read my mind at all, he asked, "You mooning over that dandy?"

He sounded so petulant, so very cross, that my contemplative state broke and fell away. Thomas would never have spoken so plainly—and Emerson Birch would. He was a different man entirely, a new possibility grown from the ashes of the last.

Sprawling onto the grass, I gazed into the bright blue sky and said, "No, but my aunt's trying to make me court him all the same."

"I could call," he said.

I rolled toward him and said, "You'd get shot."

"What does she load with? I'd survive birdshot."

My chest tightened, and I squeezed my hand. "Don't joke about it. There once was a boy I loved very much, and he's gone now—it's not funny at all."

Emerson wasn't refined like Theo; he didn't speak smoothly or eloquently, but he was keen in a way Theo couldn't hope to be. Stretching out on his side, Emerson repeated one of the first things I'd told him. "You don't handle arms."

A seam closed within me—I cannot say it was healed. But it was mended well enough, a truth said and recognized, honor paid the past, and so I nodded. Then I changed the subject, because the last one was finished.

"Tell me why Birdie can't bear the sight of you."

"You're a real romantic," Emerson complained. Dropping onto his back, he covered his face with his hat again.

Stealing his hat, I fanned my face with it lazily. "You're a stranger to me, Mr. Birch."

"I told you, call me Emerson."

I made a face at him. "I hope you didn't expect me to compromise myself just because I like looking at you, *Emerson.*"

"Well, not right away, *Zora.*"

"I think you should tell me who you are," I said. I brushed the brim of his hat against my lips and shivered. The felt was creamy soft, and warm—it felt like the promise of a kiss. "And I'll tell you who I am. Then we can both be sure we're a risk we care to take."

Swift and deliberate, Emerson reclaimed his hat and sat up. But instead of declaring me a pain, or simply riding away to simpler pleasures, he dug a handful of soil from the creek side, then reached for his unfinished apple.

He held my gaze as he bit into it, then tossed it aside.

Producing a single seed from his mouth, he pressed it into the pile in his hand and said, "This is who I am."

And he called out—not to me, to the earth. To the grasses and wildflowers and rushes all around us. To land already waking—I felt it all shiver around me. I expected the cattails to come to life, to weave around me in a cloak, and wild roses to grow a briar crown for me to wear.

They didn't. But the seed in Emerson's hand sprouted before my eyes. Fragile tendrils unfurled, first green and new, then thickening into reddish stems and fledgling leaves as they rose toward the sun. A seed became a sapling, the promise of an apple tree to come.

"Give me your hand," he said, and carefully slid the burgeoning tree into my palm. Then he raised his gaze to mine again, and he said pointedly, "It'll need watering."

Full of wonder, I stroked the newborn leaves with my fingertips. "Extraordinary. A miracle, even."

Emerson stroked his thumb against mine, and I think he meant to say something.

But I interrupted, gentle with him because I suspected he was raw and new as this apple tree in my hand. "But I want to know *you*. Your thoughts and your philosophies, your flaws and your scars. You make my blood run again, and don't be mistaken—I'm going to be very sorry when you leave today and I haven't kissed you. But you must be more than novelty."

Silent for a long moment, Emerson seemed weighed with thought, some struggle on his brow. Inside, I wavered, because I had spoken my heart plainly—I did want his hands on my face, his lips tenderly on mine. But I couldn't bear to fall for him only to discover later that the magic was all we had.

Finally, Emerson let go of my hand, and I admit, I despaired. But he pushed his hat back on his head and stood, offering a hand to me. I took it, and he pulled me rather more close than he should have, but I forgave him that when he said, "Very, *very* sorry?"

I pushed him away with my shoulder, swallowing my laughter. "You awful thing."

"Come back Wednesday," he replied.

And for the first time in a year, I had a reason to count the days again.

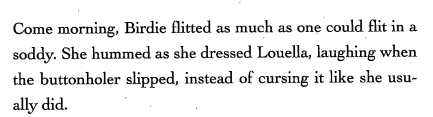

Come morning, Birdie flitted as much as one could flit in a soddy. She hummed as she dressed Louella, laughing when the buttonholer slipped, instead of cursing it like she usually did.

"Just fry some of those eggs," Birdie told me. "There will

be biscuits and coffee when we get there, I imagine, and we'll spend the rest of the day sewing or cooking. Nobody's going hungry today."

I nodded, cutting off the tiniest slice of salt pork to grease the pan. Birdie's excitement seeded the atmosphere, and I couldn't help but share it. I had heard of a barn raising but never seen one. I understood it was half frolic, half Herculean feat—a great deal more would happen than just the building of a barn.

The men would raise the walls, hopefully by nightfall, with boys running their errands. We women would cook and can and, most importantly, trade information. No doubt there would be news from back east, as well as clever recipes and tricks we'd learned on our homesteads.

And what made me tremble was knowing it would be West Glory's first chance to hire me as their springsweet. The notices had been up long enough to draw interest. We'd know by sundown if anyone thought my gifts might be worth two dollars a scry.

Straightening, Birdie gave Louella a little push. "Take your apron and go pick me four green tomatoes, the biggest you can find." Then to me, Birdie said, "If we slice them thin and fry them, we should have a respectable enough dish to offer."

"I'm sure it will be fine." I nodded, taking an egg and cracking it swiftly. I started to reassure her that they couldn't expect more than what we had to offer, but instead I screamed.

A fleshy, bloody mess quivered in my pan. It was an awful thing, contorted and foul smelling, and I clapped a hand over my mouth.

Far more sensible than I, Birdie plucked the pan up and emptied the mess directly into the fire. She said without accusation, "I take it you didn't candle those eggs."

"I brought them in fresh last night!" I pointed to the rest lying in the bowl and looking like innocents when plainly, horrifying monsters lurked within. "How could they have turned already?"

Birdie glanced at the heavens, perhaps begging strength. "They're fertilized. I'd say by the look of them, they would have been chicks in another two weeks."

Opening the front door, I fanned myself with it, but my stomach roiled again and again. Honestly, I wanted to compose myself. I wanted very much to smooth myself over, but no amount of reasoning within soothed me. Reason could hardly contend with the grip of raw, base horror.

With no time for my dramatics, Birdie plucked up the bowl of eggs and shoved them into my hands. "I suggest you go dispose of these."

I thrust them away from my body, holding them at arm's

length. I'm sure my panic came through quite clearly when I asked, "How?"

"Put them in the compost," Birdie said, pouring salt in the frying pan to scrub it clean. She moved so efficiently that what she said next sounded reasonable on first consideration. "Break them up with a stick so they don't explode."

But only nearly.

"Explode?!"

"Zora!" Birdie put the pan down hard. "Quit being a hysterical ninny. We still need breakfast, and we've got a long walk ahead of us."

How ashamed I was at that moment. I kept my tongue and slipped outside, still carrying the bowl as far from me as I could manage.

Of all the things to set me to screaming like a child, it had been nothing reasonable. No, I could endure any number of trials—whole weeks' worth of meager meals, dirt floors and robberies, forced courtship and apparent abandonment—but I had been reduced to terror by bad eggs.

I let Birdie and Louella walk ahead of me, which was some feat considering how short Louella's legs were. Perhaps I thought to indulge in sullenness, and to be fair, I kept quiet for the whole of the walk. But once I caught sight of the barn raising, I couldn't bear to sulk anymore.

By my estimation, the Baders were doing quite well. Their house was made of gleaming new lumber, the windows glass, and the door fitted with a screen to let air through during the day. Fencing marked off part of their plot, protecting several cows and four spindly calves.

I noted a chicken coop, and a hog run, a pony cart, and a plow. They had tamed the prairie for a mile at least, a wheat field still green and tender stretching toward a copse of trees in the distance. That land was especially green, no doubt lining the creek that snaked through their property and ours.

But that wasn't their only water. They boasted a new metal pump beside the house—drawing water from the depths, no doubt it rose pure and clean and clear. They had claimed a very lucky piece of land in the run, indeed. Plenty of water, plenty of good earth.

Now I understood why Birdie had fretted about slicing our green tomatoes thin. In Maryland or Oklahoma, we all did our best to keep up appearances, but how could we seem anything but poor neighbors compared to all this?

"All right, we're here," Birdie said. "Knock that puss off your face."

It seemed she and Mama both possessed a preternatural sense of all things occurring behind them at all times. Once, when I was very small, I had stuck out my tongue at the back of Mama's head, and she promptly sent me to stand in the corner.

Since I could only imagine what sort of punishment Birdie might visit on me for the same, I put on a smile as we walked into the cloud of West Glory women spread across the lawn.

"Birdie, look at you," a ginger-haired woman said, already opening her arms to pull her in. "And look at those tomatoes. They came in early! What's your secret?"

"Prayer," Birdie replied. Then she directed the woman toward me. "Caroline, this is my niece Zora. Zora, this is Caroline Edwards. She's the one who keeps me in laces and crinolines to stitch."

I offered my hand. "It's good to meet you, Mrs. Edwards."

"Likewise, I'm sure. I'll have to introduce you to my nephew," Mrs. Edwards said, pulling Birdie toward the heart of the ladies on the lawn.

"She's got a beau," Birdie said, casting me a look that dared a denial.

Though I'd hardly contradict an elder in mixed company, I simply answered with a smile. Theo wasn't my beau, but if it kept Mrs. Edwards from foisting her nephew on me, I thought I could, this once, let the lie stand.

In quick order, Mrs. Edwards managed to introduce both Birdie's early tomatoes and me to what seemed like a hundred smiling women. Almost all of them—all but the children, it seemed—were married, and when I looked toward the men as they started work on the barn, I realized we were quite outnumbered.

I watched them spreading out, selecting tools and considering a barn that, at the moment, was hardly more than a skeleton. They looked like geese, a flock of white muslin shirts and dark trousers. I was entirely amused, however, to see a shock of emerald green among them.

Theo had rolled up his shirtsleeves and bound his hair back, and it seemed that his waistcoat was cotton, a concession to the day's labor. Still, he seemed too rarefied by half among them.

Beside Emerson, he positively gleamed.

My heart jumped twice, once in seeing Emerson, and the second in seeing him approach Theo. But whatever words they shared, they were pleasant enough. Theo's smile never faded, and Emerson gestured comfortably, as if they were old friends indeed.

I was surprised to see how closely matched they were in

height, for Emerson seemed impossibly tall when I looked up at him, and I'd never had that impression of Theo. They were a strange pair—refined and rough but both, I realized, entirely beautiful in their own ways.

"Already goggling at the boys," Mrs. Bader said, slinging an arm around my shoulders.

She, like Birdie, was hardly older than I was—I guessed at most a few years, because she had twins, three years old, rolling around the lawn with Louella.

Her pert nose crinkled when she smiled, and she leaned her head toward mine. "Do you see that handsome devil there with the goatee? That's my husband."

It was charming, how infatuated she seemed to be with him—and admirable. I followed the line of her gaze and then laughed when I realized said husband was stretching himself on the barn frame, showing off for his pretty young wife. "You're a very lucky woman, Mrs. Bader."

"Fff, call me Suzannah," she said. She tugged me along, offering conspiratorially, "And come help me can. It's pickles and relish today—that's not hard at all. *And* we've got the best view of the raising."

I hated canning. It was tedious, precision work that just as often ended in an explosion as it did in a good bottle of preserves. But Suzannah had a lively air to her, her brightness refreshing. And it was good, I mused, to see new faces and hear new voices. To do new chores while enjoying the sunshine and, I admit, the view.

"Now," Suzannah said as she handed me a cloth, "while I get this to boiling, tell me everything interesting about you."

Sitting on the little wood stool by the fire, I started wiping the lids clean. My gaze drifted back to the barn, where nails were finally set to wood and hammers began to drum. "Well, I'm from Baltimore. I haven't got any brothers or sisters . . ."

"I heard you rode into town first thing of a morning with Emerson Birch," she said, cutting directly to gossip I had no idea had been circulating. "Tell me if I'm prying, but where on earth did he find you?"

"On the road," I said, choosing my words carefully. "I had meant to walk to town, but he spared me that."

"I see, I see," Suzannah all but chirped. She kept her voice low, a confidential sort of tone. "The coach came in but an hour late, and you didn't turn up until morning, so we were wondering . . ."

Bright spots of heat stung my cheeks. Finding a very stubborn spot to scrub, I measured my answer. "I had gotten quite a ways on my own. By the time Mr. Birch—"

Giggling, Suzannah repeated teasingly, "*Mr.* Birch. So

formal! But go on, go on. I'm sorry. I'll button my lips right now."

I could barely remember where I'd left off. "Ah, well, I . . . It was dark, so he took me home."

"He didn't!"

Leaning toward her, I insisted, "It wasn't untoward in any way whatsoever! He . . . he gave me his bed, and he—"

"Slept on the floor at your side?" Suzannah puffed up with a delighted breath.

I do honestly believe if I'd had a pin, I could have popped her. And the worst of it was that she didn't have a hint of maliciousness. Though I couldn't trust she wouldn't repeat my story, as she was entirely a stranger, I got the impression that she was simply starved for entertainment.

But I lied—and I don't know if it was to spare Emerson or Birdie or even my own vain self—but I looked into Suzannah's sparkling brown eyes and said, "Oh no. He took the rifle and slept in the buckboard."

"Did he really?" Suzannah brushed her skirts back and tossed another stick on the fire. She seemed just as delighted with that answer as she would have been with a more salacious admission.

I nodded, offering her the box of cleaned lids. "Yes, and then he carried me straight to my aunt's in the morning."

Suzannah sighed, the sigh of a thoroughly satisfied gossip. "What a story; you should marry him so you can tell your grandchildren how you met. Or maybe that's what I'll tell my grandchildren. They won't know the difference!"

Gently extricating myself, I said, "I'm going to check on my cousin, I'll be right back."

"I'll be right here," Suzannah sang, and I didn't doubt her one bit.

~~~~~~

As I worked my way through the stations, I felt myself stripped inch by inch. Though all the women here had come from somewhere else, every one of them had developed a directness that both fascinated and terrified me.

"Now, you're the one who does the water witching," Mrs. Rubert said, catching me between stations.

She was an older woman, her face gently lined and her hair steel gray. She wore it loose, the way the little girls did, only the sides pinned back with jet combs. On account of her age, I felt duty bound to sit with her a moment, which meant I found myself basting quilt squares as I talked.

Threading a needle, I nodded. "Yes, ma'am. Do you need a well?"

"Me? No, pet, I live in town. I'm set as set can be." She worked her end of the quilt with precise fingers. I was a fair hand at it myself, but Mrs. Rubert's stitches were so even, so straight, that I marveled. "I just wanted to know how you did it."

Reaching for a luxurious square of cornflower velvet, I thought about her question, then shook my head. "I'm not sure, to tell you the truth. When I close my eyes, I hear my own heart beating. And from there, it's as if . . . I'm listening for another one. When I finally hear it, when it matches mine, I look out and see a flickering light. That's where the water is."

Mrs. Rubert made a soft, incredulous sound. "Well, I'll be."

There was nothing I could possibly say to that, so I kept my silence and reached for another square. After a moment, Mrs. Rubert slipped her pin into the border and looked up at me. "We had a fella come through last summer, claimed to be a rainmaker."

My brows lifted in surprise. Though my ability had come to me late and strangely, hundreds claimed to share it. Throughout the country; for that matter, throughout history. But I had never heard of a rainmaker before—just as I had never heard of anyone pulling the water to the surface, though I had done that. I was sure of it.

"And was he?" I asked.

"Of course not," she scoffed. She picked up her sewing

again. "But he got a lot of fools to pay pennies to see him run up and down Main Street screaming like a stuck pig."

Though inwardly the implication stung, I managed a tart reply. "Well, at the very least, I'm a genteel springsweet. Whether my dowsings find water or no, I assure you, I'm well-mannered throughout."

Mrs. Rubert would have been entirely correct to reprimand me, but she laughed instead. "You and Birdie make some pair."

"Thank you," I said, standing carefully once I'd basted my squares in neatly. Mrs. Rubert let me drift away, and as the day turned, I sewed a little and pickled a little; I helped pack fresh pork into a salt barrel, and kissed Louella's scraped knee.

Dinner approached, and I found myself washing dishes at the pump. With so many hands frying and stirring, baking and dishing, they needed scullery far more than they needed another sous-chef. We had dirtied a mountain of pots and pans, and I despaired I'd make my way through even half before the meal was all gone.

While I sat alone at my mountain of tin and brass, smooth hands fell over my eyes. It took no effort at all to guess their owner.

"Shouldn't you be finishing the west wall with the others, Mr. de la Croix?"

Disappointed, Theo leaned over my shoulder. "How did you know it was me?"

"Lucky guess," I soothed. I shied away, so his cheek wouldn't brush mine, and I waved a hand at the lengthy chore ahead of me. "Make yourself useful, won't you?"

For once, Theo's grace failed him. He didn't even pretend to consider my request. "I'll have to get back to the men before they miss me. I just wanted to say hello."

"Hello."

Exhaling a laugh, Theo knelt down beside me. "You're a puzzle to me in every way. I think you do it on purpose."

I smiled a bit, dipping my hands in clean water, then smoothing my hair beneath my bonnet. "I do. Every morning, I get up just before dawn so I have a private hour to plan. How might I confound someone today? What trouble might I visit on some poor, unsuspecting soul?"

"I don't doubt it," Theo said. He tried to pull me into one of his dark, soulful gazes but then thought better of it. Standing instead, he slipped his hands into his pockets. "But the joke's on you today, Miss Stewart. I hope you wore comfortable shoes."

Curious, I peered up at him. "Why would you hope that?"

"Well," he said, "there are twenty-some bachelors to every single, respectable girl in these parts. And by my prudent estimation, at least eighteen of them are here right now."

"What of it?"

"I believe they all intend to stay for the dance." Leaning down once more, he caught me with a wicked smile. "And it's likewise my prudent estimation that you are the only respectable, single girl of courting age present today."

I paled. "Certainly not . . ."

Taking his leave of me, Theo dared to bow on his exit. "I do intend to cut in on a waltz. Just so you know."

He walked away, leaving me cursing under my breath. It was absolutely cruel that he'd finally discovered a sense of humor at my expense. Glaring very darkly at his back, I stewed, and I planned an escape. I very likely would have effected it, as well.

But as I went to Birdie to claim exhaustion, I saw Emerson at his buckboard. He pulled a fiddle from its case and held it up to inspect it.

Its body gleamed in the beginning lamplight, the strings catching and casting light like golden threads.

He tucked it beneath his chin to test its tune. Somehow, his rough fingers pulled the sweetest note free; the bow quivered beneath his hands, as if it begged him to draw forth one note more.

Madly, I longed to be that instrument, a yearning so sudden and so complete that I ached with it. And aching as I did, it no longer mattered if I had to waltz with the whole of West Glory—I had to stay. I had to hear him play.

I wanted nothing more than to hear him play just for me.

Thirteen

The new barn smelled sweet, of sawdust and sun-warmed pine, but ripe as well. Everyone who had worked from dawn in the prairie heat crowded inside, fripperies like bonnets and hats abandoned to comfort.

Someone had strewn clean straw, marking out the part of the barn that would be our dance floor.

Our light came in buttery patches, cast from buggy lanterns and hurricane lamps. They hung from the loft and lined the windowsills. They burned brightly, the smoke from their oil and beeswax a smudging hint of perfume.

The babies played in the stalls, and the older folks sat around the edges, to watch and chatter while the young ones, married and single, joined in the center to dance.

Emerson stood under the window, playing tuning scales

so Mr. Rubert could match the key on his mandolin. A white-haired man I hadn't met during the day stroked the pearl edge of his banjo, his foot keeping an anticipatory beat.

A little boy still in his short britches sat in quite seriously, a pair of wooden spoons clutched between his fingers. To my wonder, when the men raised their instruments and started to play, that lad kept perfect, snapping time with them.

"I wrote myself in on this one," Mr. Bader said, joking about dance cards we neither had nor needed.

The lot of us lined up in pairs, for that's what a reel called for. Our band played it rather faster than the sedate quadrilles I was used to, and soon the barn was full of boot stomping and arm swinging, clapping and unexpected laughter.

It seemed our early-morning call to work meant little — there was energy and spirit enough to dance a reel and a two-step, a Texas schottische and a double-time polka that left me gasping. Skirts of every color bloomed like flowers.

I spun from partner to partner in a dizzy, heady swirl. So many hands clasped mine, and I gazed into eyes of every shade. The speed of it dazzled me, compelled me—*just one more dance*—when I thought I could dance not one step more.

But when it came to the jig, I begged out of young Mr. Maguire's arms so I could steal a drink from the barrel and catch my breath. Dabbing my face with my kerchief, I turned to watch the spectacle. It was glorious and wild, joy lifting the roof and filling the night with song.

"Come dance," someone said, and caught my elbow. I had already grown used to the informality, passing from partner to partner as the song and the moment moved me, so I stepped into a waltz with Royal Wakes unawares, and by the time his hand fell onto my waist, I couldn't escape.

"We haven't been introduced proper," he said with a smile. He led well, with a light touch and refined steps. Nevertheless, I found him entirely repulsive.

"Miss Stewart, late of Baltimore," I said.

His smile grew as he turned me through the first chain. "Royal Wakes, late of right here. How do you do?"

Looking past him, I tried to catch another's eye, anyone's eye. I begged Emerson to raise his head, but he was lost in *The Blue Danube*, thankfully one of the faster waltzes. If they slowed the tempo, I had no hope of rescue whatsoever. As neutrally as I could manage, I said, "Fine, thank you, and yourself?"

"Pretty good, all around." He squeezed my hand, a strange light passing in his gaze. Then he pulled me closer, so much so that I felt the heat of his body radiating through his clothes. The sensation struck me as primal and unpleasant, and I leaned my head away, my only reprieve.

But to counter it, he leaned in, so his lips moved against my ear. "I just wanted to apologize for your locket."

Stiffening, I forgot to breathe. How brazen he was, to speak so openly about the wrongs he had done me, about the crimes he visited on innocent people throughout the county. Weighing my reply, I said, "If you were sorry, you wouldn't have done it."

"To be fair," he said, turning me again, "that was more Ellis than me. He's the mean one."

Lifting my chin, I said, "To let it happen is just as much a sin as doing it yourself."

"Why can't you be sweet?" he asked.

Annoyance darkened his blond brow. His grip grew tight, not so much to hurt but to warn. I knew his cut; I recognized a coward. He tagged after his brother, playing bandit. Had he not quailed when I refused to play his victim? Had he not wavered when Ellis wanted to put the gun to me?

This little man was nothing and, advice to the contrary, I refused to pay him in fear. He repaid me with a sharp squeeze that made my eyes water.

And that was the moment Theo decided to find his way to me. No doubt it was because he knew the fast waltz always preceded the slow one, but the reason mattered not at all. He was my rescue, and I was glad to see him.

He put a hand on Royal's shoulder and offered him the most charming smile. "I'm afraid this one is more vinegar than sugar. May I cut in?"

"Be my guest," Royal said.

Picking up the steps without hesitation, Theo thanked him and swirled us from Royal's company. Flicking his head back to clear the hair from his face, Theo glanced heavenward a moment before looking down at me. "What did he say to upset you so?"

My heart sank; I'd given Theo rather less credit than he deserved. And I was tired of holding in this awful secret, no matter what Birdie said would come of speaking it.

"That jackanapes is one of the men who robbed my coach. He had the gall to apologize for stealing my locket."

Troubled, Theo glanced to find Royal in the crowd again, then looked back to me. "The marshal's outside. I was just speaking with him. You should—"

"No." I pressed in, keeping my voice low. "Birdie already forbade me to speak of it, and it doesn't matter anyway. It seems most everyone knows."

"Are you serious?"

I offered a bitter smile. "It seems as long as we're being robbed by the likes of him, no one worse will come around. The Daltons murder; those two only pillage."

Affronted, Theo seemed as though he might leave me there on the floor and start some ill-advised trouble over it. But I had seen enough trouble; I knew what came of valor when it crashed into villainy.

Tenderly, I stroked his shoulder and coaxed him with a soft voice to look at me again. "It's not worth it. Please just leave it."

The music shifted, melting from a sprightly pace to a slower, more intimate one. As I had closed the last conversation unequivocally, he changed the topic with the tempo. "Speaking of Mrs. Neal, she asked if I would drive you to your appointments this week."

"I didn't know I had any."

Theo nodded, taking the half turn that would bring us to the front of the barn again. Faces swirled at the edges, a patchwork of strangers all turning sentimental on the sweet, high cry of the fiddle. "Four, at least. I admit, I accepted the task for reasons most selfish."

Of course he had.

And dancing there with him, I could see a future for the two of us. Companionable and friendly; I *had* learned to like him. We would be good friends and good partners. Perhaps we'd read poetry after dinner; he might indulge me and let me plait his hair with ribbons.

But when we turned, I caught sight of Emerson, one foot propped on an overturned crate. The lamplight bronzed his hair; it touched the soft curve of his lips and outlined the strong line of his jaw. I loved the way his suspenders cut into his shoulders; my flesh tingled with the contemplation of how smooth or how rough his cheek might be.

He played the waltz with knowing hands, strong hands — and I wanted him to play me just the same. Even if I could only say such a thing to myself, I did have to admit it.

Then, as if I had stirred him, Emerson raised his head and looked, unerringly, into me. If his fingers lingered longer on the strings, I didn't know — but I felt them. If I had a breath, it slipped from me; trembling on a vibrato note, I closed my eyes against the disappointment of losing his gaze in the next turn.

Rubbing his very smooth cheek against mine, Theo murmured, "You're never going to see me, are you?"

It took me a moment to realize what he'd said, but when I did, I felt it like a dagger. Pierced with guilt, I pulled back. There was no sense in denying it; that would heap insult on injury, neither of which he really deserved. "Theo, it's not . . ."

"Well," he said, with remarkable civility. "It was good, at least, to hear you call me by my given name this once."

He didn't turn me out on the floor—I'm not sure he had it in him to be rude, even if he wanted to be. No, he passed me back into Mr. Maguire's arms before he walked away.

Watching him slip outside without incident or commotion, with his back held straight and his head high—it was then I realized he had not lied to me.

Theo de la Croix believed in chivalry with his whole heart, and I had just broken it.

~~~~~~

Though it meant carrying Louella a long way in the dark, I was glad when the music ceased. My novelty made it difficult to sit out, but my miserable spirit made it just as difficult to dance.

Shuffling outside with Birdie, I saw her eyes turn keen. Subtly, she turned, skimming her gaze across the wagons and buggies that waited for their drivers. I had not the heart to tell her that the rich, red velvet phaeton wouldn't be there; there would be no last-minute offer of a ride home.

"Up," I murmured to Louella, shifting her onto my shoulder. I cut my way through the crowd, thinking that I would point us toward home and Birdie would naturally follow.

"Hey there, Birch," a man said—Carl, from the restaurant. *Clammy hands, weak grip,* I thought ungenerously; I had danced twice with him, but thank God none of the waltzes.

Emerson stood at his buckboard, his hat pushed far back on his head. He looked quite ready to leave but stayed nonetheless to reply. "Carl?"

Carl ground his cheroot out on his boot, wandering lazily in Emerson's direction. Even in the dark, I made out the shadow of sweat on his shirt, the sheen of it on his skin. "Everybody was real surprised to see you today. Pleased, mind you. Just surprised."

"The barn had to go up," Emerson replied.

Carl laughed, but it wasn't a friendly sound. He clapped Emerson on the back, too hard to be genial. Something percolated there—nothing I could see, but the bitter tang of it spiced the air between them. "That's the spirit. Shame we don't see you in town much."

Thunder rolled, but beneath my feet. Rubbing Louella's back, I turned, as if to find Birdie. But I can admit I was eavesdropping. Birdie made it easy, for she had disappeared.

"Jubilee's a fifteen-minute ride," Emerson said, moving to hitch his buckboard. "I get to West Glory when I can."

Pushing his hat back, Carl shook his head. "We hear rumors, you understand."

"I reckon you do."

When Emerson didn't bow or apologize, Carl pressed. "It's bad enough you're doing all your trading with those upstarts in Jubilee, but Jim Polley said you've got injuns camping your land right now. Who else are you gonna mix with?"

"Pretty much anybody," Emerson said, grabbing the iron rail to step into his buckboard. "As long as I get a fair shake and a fair price, that is. Gibson *pays* for the furs I bring him."

Something about that set a fire. Swift as a fox, Carl went after Emerson, stepping onto the wagon's sideboard and pointing an accusing finger. "You remember who you're talking to, boy."

"Mr. Birch," I called out.

I don't know what possessed me. None of it was my concern, and I had a babe in my arms. Birdie would be furious if I put her daughter in harm's way because I couldn't keep my mouth shut. But, I reasoned, what could possibly happen in the middle of a crowd, with all the eyes of West Glory around us?

Carl and Emerson both looked to me, and Emerson said, "Miss Stewart?"

Pretending a cheerful ignorance, I walked right up to his buckboard. Throwing a sugar smile in Carl's direction, I gave all my attention to Emerson when I said, "I just wanted to thank you again for that seedling. Louella's having a fine time watering and feeding it."

"Seedling?" Cloying with false sweetness, Carl reached out to pet one of Louella's curls. Uncharitably, I turned before he could.

"That's right. Our future apple tree—the only one on the whole lot."

Emerson glanced to Carl, then back at me. An unfathomable shade darkened his eyes. His voice was pulled thin as taffy, and I felt that thunder again, rolling through the ground. It was a faint tremor, just enough sensation to give me goose bumps. "You've got it in full sun, I hope."

"Oh no," I lied. "Was I supposed to? I didn't realize."

Emerson pressed his tongue into his cheek. "A tree makes its shade; it doesn't grow in it."

Shifting Louella on my hip, I said, "Can I move it, do you think? I don't want to murder the poor thing."

Perhaps realizing that I had a great number of questions for Emerson, Carl cut him an ugly look, then bobbed his head at me. "Beg pardon, Miss Stewart, I've got to go borrow a candle off Mrs. Bader. Pleasure dancing with you."

"Likewise," I said, smiling brightly until he walked off. Then I turned to Emerson, lowering my voice, "Are you all right?"

"Fine," Emerson said. "I can handle Carl Tucker."

I raised a brow. "As can I."

After a skipped beat, when his face smoothed and he peered at me as if I were some vexing creature he couldn't quite place, Emerson finally sat up. Tipping his hat, he said, "I enjoyed the chance to play, thank you."

Confused, I almost asked him if he'd gone a bit funny in the sun. Then I realized he wasn't quite looking at me, and I turned to see my Aunt Birdie almost at my shoulder.

"Good evening, Mr. Birch," Birdie said. She took Louella from my arms, soothing her when she woke with a start. "Thank you for the music tonight; it was lovely."

"Just what your niece came to say," he replied. "Thank you both. Much obliged."

With a tight smile, Birdie stepped back. "Come on, Zora. Time to go."

There would be no arguing with that. Taking the lantern that hung from Birdie's fingers, I followed. The long, odd day weighed my shoulders down; it was a strange, submissive relief to be told what to do.

Then, behind me, Emerson called, "I'll give your regards to Miss Enid, Zora."

Swallowing the sharp tang of subterfuge, I only waved in reply. Could Birdie see through me? Did she know Emerson and I intended to meet again, secretly, on his way back from Enid Station?

"Who's Miss Enid?" Birdie asked—and at the same time, answered my query.

I squeezed the lantern handle tight to steady my hand. Though I should have felt a measure of it, I told her, without shame, "A friend from Watonga; she might need a well."

"Mmm," Birdie said.

And we said nothing more on our long walk home across the nighttime prairie, nothing but a candle and our bravery to keep us.

～～～～～

I had found most of my days in Oklahoma Territory exhausting enough to easily invite sleep. Certainly, the barn raising should have left me dozing on my feet.

Instead, I lay in the ponderous dark, trying to make out the shape of the stove, the oil-papered windows, anything at all to look at, to cut the anxious tangle of thoughts in my head.

I thought I'd been very still, lying as I always did, like an Egyptienne: arms folded on my chest, and legs crossed at the ankles. It was the only way we three could sleep, really—the pallet on the floor was only as big as Birdie's widest quilt.

But Birdie nudged me and said, very low, "What's the matter with you? Ants in your britches?"

"I can't sleep."

"Obviously." Slowly, carefully, Birdie lifted the covers so she could roll on her side without displacing them. This little shifting stirred Louella, who sat up just long enough to rattle off a mouthful of nonsense before dropping down to slumber once more.

Birdie waited until Louella's breath evened, then she said to me, "You need to try. It's going to be a long couple of days for you, duck."

Covering my mouth to keep the sound inside, I nonetheless groaned. Four appointments to find water—now appointments I'd have to walk to keep. I'd forgotten about them entirely.

Four appointments, eight dollars. That was half a cow or staples for a month or enough rose-print calico for the three of us to each have a new day dress. Birdie made eight dollars a month with her sewing; in two days, I could improve our circumstances immeasurably.

The weight of that much responsibility pressed my breath away and left me struggling in the dark. My throat hurt, as if it strained to stopper my emotions. Rolling toward Birdie in the dark, I whispered plaintively, "I had to dance with Royal Wakes tonight."

"I know. I'm sorry." She put her hand on my cheek, but it didn't comfort me the way it would have if Mama had done it. Perhaps because she went on to say, "It's hard to keep still when you want to shout, but you're a good girl for going along."

It was misguided comfort, because it crystallized for me so many trembling discontents I'd felt of late. As inspiring as the sky was here, as proud and strong as my Aunt Birdie was, we did a frightening lot of looking away. We worked that patch of garden because it was our freedom but locked the doors tight and held our tongues because we lived on this land alone.

The conflict of our very existence stuck in me like a thorn, the prick of it pushing ever deeper.

Somehow, looking for a new world, for a life of service, for days of good works, I had instead come to a place where it was usual — it was *expected* — to ignore sins and grievances and injustices just to get along.

Beautiful land stretched in every direction; here on the plains, I had learned to feel the rhythm of my body, its connection to the waters that flowed through the earth. I had come all this way to discover my own magic, my own weaknesses — my own strength.

And now it was a tide coming in, crashing against rocks, etching permanent scores with every beat. I felt no keening desire to run back to the city and my mother's kitchen. But the plans I'd made in my parlor—newspapers spread, western fantasies filling my head—they had dissolved.

Birdie had been right. I *had* run away. To a place that existed in thrilling newspaper serials and fantasy and nowhere else; and there, in the real dark of the Territories, with real lives moving around me, depending on me—

I was afraid.

Fourteen

As I filled Aunt Birdie's basin for the morning's water, a beating of hooves caught my attention.

Slipping from beneath the yoke, I came round the front of the house to see Theo and his fine phaeton approaching. The sun burned behind him, a very dark Apollo indeed.

I went to meet him, a coil of shame tightening inside me. He looked not at me but beyond. Even when he spoke, he addressed the soddy or the horizon or the stormy clouds thereon—anything but me.

"You should hurry and get your bonnet. The Polleys are expecting us just after breakfast."

Wrapping my arms around myself, I tried to step closer. But even with my hip at the step, the phaeton rose high above me. I had to tip my head back and speak aloud, instead of offering the confidential murmur I intended. "You don't have to do this; it's far too much to ask—"

"I made a promise to Mrs. Neal," he said, twisting the reins around his hands. "I'm a man of my word."

Rather than argue it, I simply nodded and headed inside. I took my bonnet from the peg on the wall and said, "Mr. de la Croix is here." Suddenly his formal name lay on my tongue like ashes, but I had no right at all to call him Theo, either.

Unaware of my internal distress, Birdie brightened. She shooed Louella outside with a pat on the bottom and took me by the elbow. Instead of hurrying she measured our pace.

"Mrs. Bader is keeping lunch pails for the two of you, so make sure to drive past to fetch those. You'll see the Polleys this morning and the Stricklands this evening. They're keeping you the night, so they'll only pay a dollar fifty. First thing in the morning, you'll see the Johnsons, and then you'll finish up at Edgar Larsen's place."

"Wait, wait—I'm staying over?" I asked, stopping her. "How will I get to the Johnsons'?"

Birdie patted my arm, briefly distracted as she watched Louella try to climb aboard the phaeton. Instead of pulling her up, Theo took her to pet Annabel Lee while he waited. Dragging her gaze back, Birdie blinked, then remembered my question. "Mr. de la Croix will drive you, of course. He'll be staying as well."

Stunned, I stared at her openly. "Have you gone mad?"

"Do pay me some credit, Zora. The Stricklands are an older couple and above reproach. As long as you behave, it's no matter at all."

Perhaps not to *her*, but my knees softened, as if good bone had suddenly become gelatin. Folding inwardly, I glanced at Theo again, then said, "Shouldn't I take Louella? You won't get very much done with her underfoot."

"I managed before you got here, and I'll manage when you're gone." Then Birdie's tone changed—she grew thoughtful and turned her back to the phaeton, as if we needed to press into an alcove for privacy. "If he asks you to marry him, Zora . . . well, I can't make you say yes. But think long and hard, little girl. That is a good, honorable man, and you could do worlds worse."

It wasn't the intimation of a proposal that burned—for I knew after last night, no proposal would come. It was the way Birdie steeled herself to say it; the preciseness of her teeth, biting out each word. That she called me "little girl" instead of "duck," that her green eyes flashed away from mine—

I wanted to gather her up and stroke her hair; I wanted to plot with her and remind her she wasn't old, that all wasn't lost. I wanted to matchmake and grant wishes—if I could have, I would have given her my place.

But I could do none of that; all the magic I knew in the world lay dead or beneath the prairie and could do nothing to change the path of destiny. So instead, I pressed my brow against her temple and said, "I'll think on it, I swear."

The moment hung like a soap bubble, then burst. Birdie whipped around, all efficiency again. Striding away from me, she greeted Theo and swept Louella into her arms. Whatever words they exchanged were pleasant enough, for she smiled, and so did he.

I ruined it all by walking toward them, to take Theo's hand and a seat beside him in the phaeton.

The dawn of two long days had begun.

~~~

"Do you know what I've missed since coming here? Books. I do miss reading, don't you?"

Clutching at the hem of my apron, I offered the only thing I could think of, to begin a conversation. Though dawn crept over the prairie in a glorious blaze of crimson light, and the clouds stacked so high as to resemble mountains, the dry silence in the phaeton dulled it all.

Theo didn't answer straightaway, but he did answer. It would have been rude not to. "I brought several, actually."

With no small hint of desperation, I seized on that. "Did you? Which ones?"

"*The Phantom 'Rickshaw,*" he said. A muscle ticked in his exquisite jaw, as if it took monumental effort to speak at all. "*The Wanderings of Oisin.*"

"I was reading *A Study in Scarlet* before I came—"

Theo cut me off. "I don't care for mysteries."

All right, then. Winding back to his books, I said, "Kipling's very good, though."

"I like him well enough."

Having this terrible, stilted exchange with him only reminded me of how good he was at conversation when he wished to be. With a sigh, I folded and unfolded the edge of my apron and gazed at the lands spread before me.

There were flashes of jackrabbits, and an occasional butterfly, but mainly grass. Shades of green and of gold, tall and short, swaying in the wind, stretching to infinity. It felt like desolation, a world pulled away from my edges.

"Could I say something?" I asked suddenly.

At that, Theo did look at me. Smooth as granite, impassive as Roman marble, he said—not unkindly—"I do wish you wouldn't. I've never seen the fascination with dwelling on unpleasantries."

My lips curved to say "But I met you in a graveyard!" but I forbade them. He had a right to his sore feelings, and I had no particular right to enjoy the drives to homesteads unknown. No one had what they wanted, and in a perverse way, that seemed fair.

To make the miles pass, and to keep myself from turning too inward, from thinking too hard on the past or my situation, I cast my gaze across the waving fields and reached for the water that fanned out beneath the crust.

Faint shimmers danced like sprites; a stream in the distance was a silver ribbon lacing the land and the sky. I caught my breath when a wide river opened up, so vivid I thought we would splash through it. The clear, sweet taste of it filled the air, the cool kiss of its mist settled on my skin. Perhaps it was imaginary, but it was vivid all the same.

I wondered if Amelia had ever toyed with her sight this way; if it felt native to her, like a coil of her own hair or the particular tilt of her eyes. As I let the magic drain away, back into me, or to its ephemeral place in the earth, I sighed.

Most likely she hadn't—*I* urged her, I delighted in her gift and made a show of it—I'd been quite comfortable in her magic, but had she? I'd never asked. And now I never could.

The phaeton stopped with a jolt. It shook me out of my thoughts, and I looked around, a bit confused. I had lost some time in my reverie, it seemed, for we had come out of the desolation to a little farm sprung up in the middle of the wild.

Not as rich as the Baders', but far better appointed than Birdie's homestead, the Polleys' plot was all house and crops, from what I could see. And there was a pump at the corner of the porch. I didn't know why they needed me.

Theo came around to help me from the phaeton, then walked me to the Polleys' front door. He was stiff as a butler, a handsome, well-formed sentinel and nothing more.

Raising my hand, I glanced at him, but he didn't return the look. So I knocked and made myself pleasant when a lovely woman, round as an apple, opened the door to me.

"I'm Zora Stewart," I told her. "The springsweet."

~~~~~~

Water for the house was no matter at all, I discovered.

Jim Polley walked us the length of his land, waving birdish little hands as he explained. "We're doing all right at the front, but look here." He slapped at a corn stalk that had browned at the edges. "Going short of rain this year, my back forty's dying."

My back ached to water a plot just big enough to feed three; we had walked so far, there was nothing but wheat and corn to consider. I didn't see what another well could do here—I had to admit, I understood nothing of the business of working the land. "You do know I can't call the rain."

"Who can?" Mr. Polley said, a hiccup in his laugh. He stopped, pointing me toward an oasis just in the distance. "See there? That pond belongs to the Gibsons. Not a damned thing I can do about that, either."

Shifting beside me, Theo finally spoke. "But is there something Miss Stewart can do for you?"

Mr. Polley smiled at me winningly. He was a handsome man, with chestnut hair that fell in waves and hazel eyes that reflected the same gold and green shades of his fields. But his prettiness paled when he lowered his voice.

"Maybe I'm wrong, but I'm thinking a spring feeds that pond. Now, if you could tell me if that spring's on *my* land, that'd be worth two dollars at least."

To cover my dismay, I said, "I do beg your forgiveness, Mr. Polley, I know it's crass to speak of money— nevertheless, I must. It's two dollars, whether I find water for you or not."

Reaching into his pocket, Mr. Polley pulled out a few worn bills. Counting off two, he handed them to Theo— then held another up, as if I were a dog and he tempted me with a savory treat. "I could irrigate a lot of land with a spring. I bet you and your aunt could do with some cheap flour and cornmeal grown right nearby."

His inky voice stained me. Standing there with a fixed smile and a dollar bill under my nose, I couldn't help but remember that it was Jim Polley who told Carl who came and went on Emerson's land. That was the full measure of this man — concerned only with aggrandizing himself, wearing the mantle of *concerned citizen* to justify it.

My insides boiled and I bowed to him, taking a step back. I'd paid to see enough spiritualists in Baltimore that I could put on a truly spectacular show.

Stamping my feet, I threw my arms out and my head back. Somehow, I found the nerve to pull a scream from my throat. It went on and on, an awful, raw sound that I hoped haunted Jim Polley all his days.

There was a feral sweetness in whipping myself around like that. A vicious pleasure in breaking out of my skin and screaming with no propriety to temper it. No wonder so many made an art of it — how glorious was it to forget to be a lady and to be every wild thing contained in my heart.

Snapping myself out of that posture, I grabbed Mr. Polley's shirt, twisting the muslin as I rolled my eyes at him like some mad beast.

"There!" I cried, shoving him away from me. I pointed to

the middle of his fields, far from the Gibsons' property line. "Dig there, sir! Dig deep!"

Mr. Polley spun like a weathervane, following the line of my finger. "Right there?"

With feigned exhaustion, I staggered away from him. Clasping a hand to my forehead, I motioned them from me, putting much space between me and Mr. Polley. *"I'm weary with witching and fain would lie down.* Thank you, sir. Thank you, kind sir."

"I should see to her," Theo said, and bless him, he took that third dollar right out of Mr. Polley's hand.

He hurried to my side, but there was no gentleness in the way he took my elbow and hurried me along. And I myself trembled with nervous energy, the aftershock of the performance leaving me jittery and unsettled.

It wasn't until the phaeton was in sight that Theo deigned to speak to me. Incredulous, he spat low, quoting the very same ballad I had just incorporated in my play-acted dowsing. *"I've been to the wild woods, mother, make my bed soon."*

That spark of recognition delighted me. With Mrs. Polley on the porch, I didn't dare smile. But I looked up at Theo and nodded faintly. "You really are very good with poetry, Mr. de la Croix."

Eyes blazing, Theo looked as though he wanted to shake me. But ever the gentleman, he instead stood straight and let the hard line of his jaw and brow remonstrate me. "Forgive me for speaking out of turn, but I'm appalled that you would help that man commit such a nefarious deed."

"I didn't." I took the money and tucked it in my pocket. "He'll dig to Peking before he finds water there."

Theo said nothing. He moved not at all. So I thrust my hand at him to make him help me into the buggy. And there I waited for him to round and climb in the other side. Flickers and sparks ran beneath my skin, only slowly leaching away as we drove on. But it was not until the Polleys' farm was well behind us that I turned to him.

"Please believe me," I said, putting a hand on his shoulder. "I would never do something so awful."

Glancing at my hand, then up at me, Theo appraised me darkly. "You dissemble so easily. And I knew that. That kiss at the fountain was a lie, too—how could I forget?"

I folded myself and turned away. It was a hard thing, to know so clearly that I was hardly an innocent—that I had done wrong. That I had been selfish and hurt him because I'd thought only of myself. Though my throat burned, both from screaming and now from damming emotion, I spoke nonetheless. "I used you badly, and I truly am sorry."

After a moment, Theo said, "That I believe. Thank you."

"Birdie is nothing like me, you should know."

It looked as though Theo intended to answer—his lips

parted, and he leaned slightly toward me. But the baffled line at his brow faded, and he recovered his smooth expression. Urging Annabel Lee on, he didn't reply, but the silence was no longer awkward.

It was contemplative.

Fifteen

The Stricklands were blessedly simple. They were, as Birdie said, an older couple with a modest home on their plot. They had no ambitions for a working farm—they had just enough to keep them comfortably, and that was their goal.

When we arrived, Mr. Strickland led me to the well out back. It was built sturdily with stones and had a good crank to pull the water up.

All he wanted to know was if it was in the right place. I suspected he knew—I likewise suspected my aunt had plotted this stop to enforce courting, more than to earn a dollar and two bits.

But I looked in earnest and reassured him he'd struck

water good and true. With that, he clapped a hand on Theo's back and walked him off to talk about whatever manly things he thought wouldn't interest me, leaving me to start dinner with Mrs. Strickland.

She was kind, and her kitchen was generous. She had a black iron stove, much like my mama's, and wide counters to work on. With windows thrown open to let in the breeze, and the richness of real white flour dusting my hands, I made pleasant conversation with the lady of the house.

"All our lives," Mrs. Strickland told me as we rolled biscuits at the table, "we hustled and bustled and kept up with New York City. Last year, he had a spell that scared us both, and he said to me, 'Missus, let's go west.'"

Reaching for the bowl of flour, I dusted my part of the table again and offered her a smile. "Just like that?"

"Yes, girlie, and here we are." She breathed deep, warm with a satisfied smile. "Here in the Lord's country, just the two of us, content as can be."

It was sweet, the way she stole looks at Mr. Strickland. To my eyes, he was a bit bald and a bit wide, his skin mottled and his hands gnarled. But whatever Mrs. Strickland saw made her smile.

"You're very lucky," I said softly.

Without pretense, Mrs. Strickland asked, "What do you think of that boy out there?"

"He's not for me," I answered. Gently, I rolled the dough out again. I tore a little corner off and popped it in my mouth. It was rich with butter and salt, two things I'd never before considered luxuries. "And I'm not for him; we agree on that."

Mrs. Strickland gave me a dusty pat as she went by, checking the heat of her stove. "Then I won't bother leaving you two alone with dessert."

It was strange how much a relief that was. That there was no worrying or troubling over it, that any way I felt was perfectly reasonable. Set free for the moment, I relaxed and let myself enjoy the evening.

It was a good dinner and a pleasure to sleep in a grass ticking bed. It smelled of the prairie, sweet and green. For the first time since I'd slept in Emerson's bed, I was warm and comfortable, and I dreamed the whole night through.

Come morning, Mrs. Strickland warmed last night's biscuits and spooned white gravy on our plates to soften them. She even packed us off with a few apiece, to have on the road.

Apparently, Mr. Strickland had shared some fineness with Theo, too, for he smelled of cherry pipe tobacco and sat more easily beside me. Though we made no particular conversation, things simply felt better.

It was a beautiful day.

~~~~~~~

At the Johnsons', I finally had earnest work to do.

They'd been hauling water from a nearby stream. The winter past, Mr. and Mrs. Johnson both had to do the chore, because the water froze and had to be hacked apart and let to melt.

The burgeoning curve of Mrs. Johnson's belly told me all I needed to know—this winter, she would hardly be fit to take a pick to frozen streams, and soon they would need rather more water to get through their everydays.

I relished calling up the visions for them; I made no show of it at all. I simply reached for that pulse and led them to the exact spot when I found it. Their well would be a hundred steps from their back door.

"That wasn't very impressive," Theo said unexpectedly.

Stretching in the seat beside him, I yawned. "The truth doesn't need embellishment."

"How did you learn to do it?"

"I didn't." With a shrug, I settled beside him again. "I thought I could, and I did."

"But how did you even conceive its possibility?"

He sounded like a little boy trying to puzzle out a riddle. I would have been glad to give him an answer, though I suspected he'd have remained unsatisfied. Stretching my feet out, I pointed my toes, then relaxed once more. "I had a friend once; she saw the future."

"She doesn't anymore?"

Closing my eyes, I said, "She's no longer with us."

Theo made a sympathetic sound and took my hand gently. He neither petted nor stroked me; there seemed to be no intention in it at all but to comfort. "Forgive my curiosity."

"She's a fond memory, and I'm glad for it," I told him. "I'm fine now."

And mostly, I meant it. There would always be a tender part of me, unhealed from that disastrous summer. How could it be anything but, with my first love and my first best friend, and so many others, given to death in it?

But my mother's words came back to me, clearer than ever, and finally I believed her—I was alive. It was no longer a curse, no matter how complicated things had become here.

I leaned against Theo's arm and said idly, "It wasn't just

her. She was the first, of course. But now there's me — and I know someone who can whisper a tree to life."

"I hope you won't take this with any malice; I don't mean any," Theo said. He knitted his brow, a faint smile at the corner of his lips. "But your life is very strange."

"Thank you, sir. I was entirely unaware."

Returning his hand, I stretched beside him once more. The sun had dipped low; we had driven across the whole of Oklahoma Territory, it seemed. I was glad that we had but one more call between here and home.

I would tell Birdie that Theo hadn't proposed — it was the truth. And then I would tell her that she had to let Emerson come to court. My time lingering in shadows had ended. Wherever I would go, whatever I would do — I would do it deliberately.

How funny that despite my sorry history of making plans, I made them nonetheless.

~~~~~

Edgar Larsen met us at the edge of his property.

Gaunt in the cheeks and dark beneath his eyes, he had plainly suffered for the land he claimed in the run. He shook Theo's hand, and I had to hold back a shudder when he shook mine. It was like holding a bag of bones, and I struggled to offer him a smile.

"Pleased to meet you," I forced myself to say.

When he let go to run his fingers through his white-blond hair, I was grateful. He nodded; it seemed he was too exhausted even for pleasantries. Leading us toward the small cabin, he said, "Get you all some coffee?"

Theo and I both demurred. Pressing a hand to my chest, I said, "It's much appreciated, but it's getting late and we've been on the road two days now."

"Right," he said. He stood there, then creaked to motion again. His pale skin was chapped red, and beneath his shirt, I could make out every awful knob of his shoulders when he turned to lead us to his well.

Like Mr. Larsen, the land was withered. Only very low grasses grew here, and even then, sparsely. The rest was marred with scars, long, bald runs of dust that swirled round and round with nothing to tether it.

He'd built the well nicely, a strong stone circle with an inset lid. But when he raised that lid, he released a rank scent. Slick and moldering, it fouled the air, though Mr. Larsen seemed, at this point, resigned to it.

"It's been off a while now," he explained.

When he moved to pull the bucket up, I stayed his hand. I had no need to see what would come out of a place that smelled of decay. Whatever water collected in this well, and I was sure it was only rain that occasionally filled it, it had gone stagnant. Although ashamed to think it, I was doubly glad we'd declined his offer of coffee.

"Let me see if I can find something for you," I said. I didn't need to walk out into the open expanse behind his cabin. My intent was to draw Mr. Larsen and Theo away from the wretched stink—I had walked through Baltimore alleys more fragrant.

Now my nerves jangled with need, my skin tight and parched with the yearning to be cleansed. My heartbeat pounded in my ears, a hard rush of blood that raced too fast for someone standing still. Something was wrong—I felt nothing here, just my own body, my own dry tongue in my mouth.

The well had unsettled me in ways I had hardly expected. I smiled at Mr. Larsen, though it felt plastered and stiff. "Just trying to focus. I'm a bit tired is all."

Reaching again, I sought out that well within me, that strength that had split stone and brought water to the surface at the Coles' farm. It was like digging fingers into my chest, plundering skin and plucking bones, but nothing would come. No matter the depth of my breath, no matter my earnestness, this land had no pulse.

My face grew hot, and I wandered out a little farther.

Perhaps the sunset kept me from seeing—perhaps I was overwhelmed with the resignation. I could imagine a hundred excuses, but the result was the same. We stood on barren stone.

"I can't find anything," I said helplessly. "You could get a rain barrel, or, or . . . if you know the Gibsons, they've got a spring on their land. They might let you dip from it."

Mr. Larsen dug into his pockets, pulling forth change instead of bills. Counting them into Theo's palm, he shook his head. "Believe I'm a quarter short, Miss Stewart."

"It's all right," I said, but he walked toward the house.

Theo hurried over, turning my hand in his to put the change in my palm. "You can't keep this."

"No, I didn't intend to." Pushing my hair off my face, I stared at the horizon. It had darkened, the first shades of purple twilight, but even with the coming dark, I could find not a single light in it. Dumbfounded, I murmured, "How can there be *nothing?*"

The answer was a shot. It rent a gouge in the air, echoing plaintively into the distance.

Theo grabbed me, but our animal senses knew what our thinking ones hadn't yet realized. There was no danger in this, not for us. We both turned toward it, not away—and found ourselves facing the desolate little house into which Mr. Larsen had just disappeared.

"Stay here," Theo said.

My head roared with old thunder, with an old flash. I saw splashes of red, and white skin, and the smooth, cool nothing that crept into lifeless eyes. Time couldn't dull that shock; new plans couldn't soften that horror. It was mine, and it always would be—but it didn't have to be anyone else's.

I ran after Theo, grabbing his shoulder. "No. Drive us into town. We'll speak to the marshal."

"We can't simply—"

"Yes we can!" I made him face me. "Trust me when I tell you this: it will change you. What waits in there, you'll never be clean of it."

"Zora," he said, strained.

I dug my fingers in deeper, clinging to him for his own good. "It may break you, and you don't deserve that. Not for paying me and my aunt a favor. That's not the wage of chivalry. Please."

Stricken, Theo scrubbed his hands over his face. He looked at the house, then back at me. And he struggled, his expression leaping, trying desperately to find some center. "But if he's . . ."

"There's nothing we can do for him." I took his hand, and I pulled him along, soothing as I could be with my own emotions run so ragged. "Please, walk me to the phaeton and drive us into town. Please."

Automatically, Theo took my elbow. We both walked in a daze, and I felt him hesitate beside me, deciding whether he should put me in the car and go back anyway. But he lifted me up and followed instead of going round.

"Straight to town," I told him gently, and as we pulled away, I dropped seven quarters into the dust.

Sixteen

Someone fetched Birdie to town, so while I sat in an empty restaurant, clinging to a cup of tea, the marshal spoke with her at length.

I'm not sure why it took so long to explain such a simple, terrible act. Perhaps it always did; when Thomas died, time passed in blinks and starts. It was both endless and instant, and in the beginning, all of it blessedly numb. Mr. Larsen had been a stranger to me, and I think, my victim—so the seconds passed cruelly, each one a brand on my skin.

"Zora," Birdie said, even before she got through the door. She rushed over, wrapping me in tender arms. She smelled of brown sugar and molasses; my addled mind guessed that she'd fixed baked beans for supper.

Looking up at her, I said, "I know we need the money, but I don't think I can do this again."

Birdie burst into tears, and like me, she was hardly lovely at it. Red blotches marred her skin; her tears didn't take delicate, rivulet paths down her cheeks, they spilled out, soaking her—soaking me.

Furiously, she swiped at her face, then caught mine between her hands. "To hell with the cow."

I slumped, pressing my brow to her shoulder. Soaking up her familiar warmth, I rested there, my anxiety dissolving by the moment. Her fingers played across my hair, carding the curls as she petted me. Without thought, I murmured, "You remind me of Mama."

"Good God, don't tell me that." She shook me, then turned away to wipe her face. And just that quick, she put herself back together and pulled me to my feet. "Come on, duck. Lou's sleeping in the Herringtons' wagon. I expect the mister would like to get home before midnight."

I followed her outside, drinking in the cool night air. Leaving my bonnet to hang down my back, I matched Birdie's efficient pace as we headed for the general, taking in the town after sunset.

Dark transformed West Glory. The buildings' false fronts loomed above, black as gargoyles. The only light came from the restaurant behind me and the saloon in front of me.

I saw Theo inside, an elbow on the bar, propping himself up while he talked to the marshal. I wondered if he was all right. He managed a weary smile but ordered another drink.

It was no wild scene, just dusty men hunched over glasses and cards. Perhaps it was too early for bar fights or soiled doves; more likely, they'd never come. The western adventure the newspapers back east had promised was gossamer, made of the same ephemeral stuff as fairy tales.

West Glory was a small town trying to get by in a hard land, nothing more.

~~~~~~

Two days after, I took a bucket to pick incidental berries and set off for the creek. Birdie had treated me like porcelain all morning and didn't argue when I told her I was going for a walk.

Heat trailed in wavering rivers, reflecting sky and grass, twisting them together like a kaleidoscope. There was a particular thinness to the air—it felt as though someone had opened a great oven and we had no choice but to stand beside it.

It burned the sound and life from the prairie, burrowing animals clever enough to find some relief beneath the earth, and flying creatures resting in their nests and bowers. The back of my neck prickled, with sweat and with the eeriness of a land so still and silent.

The creek offered some relief. The water whispered on the rocks, minnows flashing like silver bangles in the shallows. I sat in the reeds and unlaced my boots, leaving them behind so I could wade. Pulling my combination over my knees, I lifted my skirts high to keep both dry as I splashed along.

Crayfish zipped away from me in their backwards way, and they were lucky they were no bigger than my pinkie. Mama had a particularly good recipe for New Orleans gumbo, and I wasn't above trying to recreate it from memory.

Rocks pressed into my bare arches, the water rising above my ankles as I sloshed along. The sun had warmed the water, but the water cooled me nevertheless. And it soothed me, swirling against my skin; it whispered and elevated me, scrubbing away all the dark and the turmoil of late.

I felt it everywhere like a caress. Then, beneath that, a faint tremor. I turned, knowing I'd see Emerson between the cattails, and there he was.

"Sorry I'm late," he said.

"You can always catch up," I told him.

But instead of wading in with me, he followed me along the shore, both feet firmly on his earth. He was gold as the

prairie, his hair shining and his skin baked a deep bronze —
and beautiful in his imperfections.

He'd broken his nose once; I was sure of it. His lips were
thin and teeth flat beneath them. He was not a god walking,
no fae king slipped out of Avalon, which Theo very well
could have been. He was rough and plainspoken, and I
wanted him to be mine.

"My philosophy," he said suddenly, "is, leave me to mine,
and I'll leave you to yours."

Gathering my skirts in one hand, I reached out to catch
his with the other. Our fingers threaded together knowingly,
clasping in just the right way. Surely, he could feel my racing pulse; the gentle way he squeezed my hand is what set it
to running. "You've got but the one?"

He nodded. "There was no living with Pa after Ma died.
I was about grown, and I looked like her. I don't know why
that set him off, but it did. So I packed up my things — I fig-
ured, there's free land to be had in the Territories. I'll go
get mine."

"And here you are," I said.

"Except it's not that neat, Zo." His thumb rasped against
mine as he ordered his thoughts. The pet name was new, but
it slipped out so easily — I wondered, is that what he called
me in his mind? Had he rolled this conversation over until it
was smooth and perfect in his thoughts?

Finally, he said, "Look, the rules were real simple. You had to be eighteen. You had to run to claim your plot when the gun went off, and you had to improve the land or they wouldn't give you the deed."

"All right." I smiled at him, curious, for his expression wasn't a victorious one, and I didn't understand why. Surely he wasn't worried that his improvements weren't enough to earn his deed. "So you lined up and—"

Emerson stopped. He turned our joined hands over and kissed the inside of my wrist. It was quick, laced with a hint of desperation. Then, whatever possessed him to do it slipped away, and he seemed very himself again: blunt and matter-of-fact. "I bought a birth certificate in Philadelphia so they wouldn't turn me away."

Surprised, I wasn't sure what to say. "How old *are* you?"

"Seventeen now," he replied. He flattened his lips, as if the number annoyed him. "But that's the least of it. I walked out the night before, just to get a look, and I realized some of those lots would never grow. What was I gonna do if I got one of the dead ones?"

The day darkened around me. I knew exactly what some men would do, given a vast, lifeless expanse. "Go on."

"I had my flag and my stake, and I planted them the night before. I cheated, straight up, and they've got a word for that out here: *sooner.* That's why your aunt looks at me the way she does. Why they'd just as soon spit on me in West Glory." He pursed his lips. "All I wanted was a piece of land and a life that was my own.

"I wasn't out here three weeks before the Arapaho came through. All I had then was a tent and a fire, but I saw them put up their village in a night. A few weeks later, they brought it down again. Up and disappeared without leaving a mark. They knew where the water was, where the game was. They *knew* this land. And you know how?"

I shook my head. There was no need to say anything; I knew he'd answer his own question.

"Because it was *theirs* first. I thought I could live with that, but your aunt's right—I stole my land. It's just, she thinks I stole it from the government."

"Emerson—"

"Leave me to mine," he said sharply, "and I'll leave you to yours. I don't know that I'm staying here, Zo. But I don't know where the hell I'd go, either."

Frozen, I struggled to reply. I wanted to argue at first, because how could the government give him something it didn't own? Or wasn't it good enough to leave the Indians in peace to come and go and camp his land if they wanted?

But I held my tongue as realization set in.

For me, one day the Indian Territories became Oklahoma

Territory, and not once had I wondered at it. It was just the way it was—I'd accepted it the same way I had accepted Buffalo Bill's stories as the truth.

"So that's my philosophy," Emerson said. He let his hand slip from mine and dropped his hat on his head. "And if you think you can live with that, come back tomorrow."

"Emerson! Em! Wait!" I reached for him, but he slipped away without a backward glance.

I had asked for this exactly—I had demanded it. As I gathered my shoes and my pail, I wondered if I would have been happier throwing myself into his arms instead of learning him before I leapt. Impetuous kisses were the sweetest kind, or so poets told me—mad love was the truest sort. Was it true?

A dry, hot wind scored my face as I trudged home; the birds remained silent, the sky a voiceless blue.

I had no answer at all.

That evening, I sat by the outside fire, boiling water for baths. If I'd had something to read, there would have been light enough. But instead, I had slipped my old dance card from its hiding place. It bore its age poorly.

Stained with mud and bent from trampling, the card had

warped and no longer closed flat. The once-gleaming gold ribbon was frayed and pale, the pencil long gone. I opened the card, as I had so many times, and trailed my fingers along the worn pages. Most of the lines were blank; Thomas' handwriting haunted the rest.

Birdie came around the house, shooing Louella out of her way with a gentle nudge. Thrilled to be stripped to her combination, Louella ran to the edge of the yard, turning like a top. It didn't occur to her to be afraid of what might lurk in the dark; she cared nothing for propriety. She was unreservedly happy, spinning herself sick for no reason but she could do it.

Birdie leaned over the pot, dipping fingers in to check the temperature. She spared me a glance. "You've been quiet."

Waving the dance card at her, I said, "This time last year, I thought I knew everything."

"I've got news for you," Birdie said with a wry smile. "Every year, you know less and less. Bet you a new penny that's why old folks rock and smile all day long."

"I don't have a new penny."

"An old one will do." Birdie took the dance card, looking it over. "I'll give you one for your thoughts."

Steeling myself with a fortifying breath, I said, "I'm not going to marry Theo de la Croix. He didn't ask, and he's not going to. We're . . . friends."

There was no chill or malice to it when Birdie said, "And you're hardheaded enough to mean that."

I nodded, gazing past the fire to watch Louella play. Wobbly from her game, she dropped to the ground, tucking her little arms behind her head. She looked so serious, and for the briefest of moments, I could imagine her much older — her blond hair tamed in a chignon, her skirts to the floor. Maybe she'd lie in this same grass, under these same stars, pondering beaux and mysteries alike.

But I pushed those thoughts aside; she had time enough to grow up. It would come on fast, before she knew it — she needed to enjoy the night and the sky and running wild in her underclothes while she could.

Pulling myself back from that meditation, I looked to Birdie again. "What if you were right — "

"Take that as a given," Birdie said, teasing. Then she raised her brows expectantly, letting me finish my thought in peace.

I cleared my throat. "What if I did run away? The Territories, coming west — it's not what I expected. At all. I love you and Louella, and it's not the hard work. I don't mind hard work."

Birdie smoothed her thumb along the edge of my dance card, then fanned her face with it. "Out with it."

"I don't want to abandon you."

Handing me the card, Birdie stood abruptly. At first, I thought she might be angry; she turned away and tipped her head back, the way Mama sometimes did when she was trying not to give someone a tongue-lashing she thought they deserved. But Birdie's shoulders shook, and she was silent until she faced me again, her pink lips bitten.

"Zora," she said. She enunciated carefully, as if the words might get away from her. "Pauline asked me to keep you until you came to your senses, and Lord knows, nobody tells my sister no. You've got to understand, ducky. I don't *need* you to get by."

I exhaled a soft "Oh."

"You'd better take that the way I mean it, too." She leaned down, pressing her head to mine. Her voice was soft, a breath on my cheek. "I love you, and I'll keep you as long as you want to stay. But I'm not your anchor. Don't go making me one."

Reaching back, I tangled my fingers in her hair. I shifted my weight to lean into her, and she did the same, pressing us close and fond. I felt like a selfish thing, a foolish thing, believing that I alone kept and preserved her. Being told otherwise hurt, but in the right way—the way my head ached when I'd learned something new.

After a while, I murmured, "Thank you, Birdie."

"You're welcome." She made a kissing sound, then peeled away from me easily. Gesturing toward the pot, she said, "Now, carry that inside. I'll go wrangle Lou."

That was my Aunt Birdie—all sentiment until she wasn't. I smiled a little, just to myself, and did as I was told.

Seventeen

I had my escape to the creek planned—and then it was thwarted.

Mrs. Rubert had shown me how to make cattail relish at the barn raising. It took little more than green tomatoes, of which we had an abundance, and vinegar and sugar, which were cheap. Just at Louella's nap, I gathered the pail and fixed my mouth to promise a pound of cattail bulbs for supper.

Certainly, I could have told Birdie where I intended to go, whom I intended to meet, but I chose, instead, to keep my own counsel. The recent tragedy was reason enough to keep my head low and to go along, but in truth, it was my own contemplative state that kept me from speaking.

I hadn't lied. I wanted to touch Emerson Birch. I wanted to kiss him and feel his hands on my face. Teasing him came easily, and his barbs crackled and snapped. He was handsome, and talented—his gift with a fiddle chilled and delighted me both.

He was earth without water. I was water without earth.

But was that enough to hitch myself to him, to accompany him, when he himself couldn't say where he might go? No, the question was more elemental than that: was I running *to* him or *away* from my mistakes?

Until I knew, until I was sure, I wasn't ready to fight Birdie about it. I wanted to choose my battles, and I had no strategy to win this one yet. It would wait until I could.

"Birdie," I called, coming out of the garden with the pail dangling from my hand, "I'm going to—"

"Somebody's coming," Birdie said. A deep furrow pressed into her brow, and she crossed her arms tight over her chest. "Horseback, no wagon."

My chest tightened. Anyone we'd want to see would no doubt come hitched to a phaeton or a buckboard. Putting the bucket down, I went to stand beside her, watching as distant plumes of dust took the shape of the marshal.

Before he'd entirely stopped, Birdie marched toward him. She had a dragon's smile on—it could be mistaken for pleasant, if you didn't know the woman wearing it. "You're out a long ways, Dennis. Is something the matter?"

The marshal circled his horse, rubbing her neck to calm her. He made no move to dismount, so I thought he couldn't possibly have any news of dire import. He tipped his hat to Birdie, then to me, before saying, "Well, about that notice you put up in town."

"I'm sorry you came all this way," Birdie said. "In light of Mr. Larsen's passing, my niece and I have decided it's best if we let God sort out the water situation here in O County."

Shifting the toothpick in his mouth from one side to the other, the marshal sighed. "I wish it was that easy, Birdie. Jim Polley made a complaint this morning."

Stilling, I measured my breath. "Did he, sir? About what?"

The marshal frowned. "He says you put on some song and dance about finding a spring in the middle of his fields when there's not a drop to be had. Says he's been digging two days straight now and got nothing but a mule's grave to show for it."

"He should read our notice again," Birdie said. She caught my arm and pulled me close, petting me like some precious angel. "It's two dollars for the appointment. We never promised anybody water."

"Jim says she cheated him out of *three*." The marshal looked to me for some refutation.

Instead, I lifted my chin. "He wanted to know how he could drain the Gibsons' spring onto his land. I didn't feel moral or ethical helping him do that, so I pointed out another source I thought he could rightfully tap. I offer my sincerest apologies if he found nothing there. Was it wrong of me to accept a tip for services rendered?"

The marshal rolled his toothpick again and said, "Probably not, Miss Stewart. But it would go a long way to keeping the peace if you'd give it back."

At that, Birdie interjected. "Why doesn't he want to keep the peace with us? This little girl drove three hours from home to call on them, and she did just what she said she would."

"Yes, ma'am, I know." The marshal scrubbed his face with his hand. "I'm not saying he's right. I'm just saying calm between neighbors is best for everybody."

At that, I snapped. I hadn't earned the dollar, not honestly, and I think if the marshal had cajoled us some other way, I might have argued Birdie down and returned it. But I was tired of holding my tongue to keep the peace.

"Well, how about this, Marshal," I said briskly. "You arrest Royal Wakes for robbing my coach, and I'll give Jim Polley his tip back with interest. Unless you think Royal's already spent what he stole from my luggage."

A dark look crossed the marshal's face. "That's a serious accusation you're making, Miss Stewart."

"Oh, shut your rag box, Dennis." It was Birdie's turn to roll her eyes. "We all know what the Wakes boys get up to. Let's be plain here: Are you demanding a refund?"

The marshal pursed his lips, then said, "I don't believe so. Jim paid for her to turn up, and she did."

Turning her bright eyes on me, Birdie asked, "Are *you* filing a complaint against Royal Wakes?"

For a small, pretty creature, my Aunt Birdie could be terrifying. I didn't dare say anything but "No, ma'am."

Birdie made a satisfied sound. "All right, then. Zora, you go on about your chores. Marshal, I would invite you in, but my baby girl's napping right now, and I don't have any coffee anyway."

"That's quite all right," he said. Then, as if he had to do something to reestablish his authority, he said to me, "I'll be pulling down those notices of yours. Between Larsen dying and Polley up in arms, well . . ."

Picking up the pail, I nodded, as if he hadn't just very manfully decided what Birdie had already told him—that I was out of business and planned to stay that way. I did hope my sarcasm wasn't entirely evident when I said, "I'm ever in your debt, Marshal."

I fled before anyone could call me back.

High, dry heat beat on my shoulders, and when I reached the creek, I longed to strip off and lie in its cool waters. The current would pull the knots from my hair and the weight from my soul. I wanted to plunge deep, to bathe in haunting silence—to emerge entirely new. I would be Ophelia triumphant, floating, not drowning.

Instead, I peeled off my boots and stockings, leaving them in a heap on the shore. My spirit was disturbed, my head too full with no release. I was angry, hungry, tired— I grieved and I yearned. I hesitated.

Splashing through the creek, I soaked my skirts, though I held them high. Nimble minnows fled my path. And when thunder rolled beneath my feet, the distant trembling that announced Emerson's arrival, I turned to call to him. "You're late!"

"You're crazy," he called back. Leaving Epona to graze, he cut through the cattails and stopped, just to gape at me. "The racket you were making, I thought you were wrestling with the only gator in Oklahoma."

"Don't bait me. I haven't got the temper for it today."

Running his thumbs beneath his suspenders, Emerson took a long, appraising look at me. When his gaze rose to meet mine, he said, "What's the matter?"

"Everything!"

Holding his arms out wide, almost taunting, he said, "Well, start at the beginning."

I kicked at the water. "I don't want to! I keep going back to the beginning, but what's the beginning? I don't know how to count myself anymore. I'm uncertain, and I hate it! I was always certain before!"

Emerson rolled his shoulders. "So pick something and go with it."

"It's hardly that simple," I declared.

With infuriating calm, he asked, "Why isn't it?"

"You said yourself, you had no idea where you'd go from here," I said. "You stand there mouthing simplicity at me, and you don't know! No better than I do!"

"It's not the end of the world to guess and get it wrong."

"What a convenient philosophy," I snapped. But then I deflated, ashamed of myself. I knew I looked foolish — I was much too old for tantrums.

Hitching my skirts up a little more, I stalked back toward my boots. I would dress, I would settle myself — by force of will, I would sort myself out — such was my intention.

But an oily musk filled the air. A pungent violation, it barely registered before I understood it was a warning. That I realized too late. Uncoiling like a whip, a thick black snake struck at me. Unfurled, it struck again.

Too startled to scream, I staggered ashore. All my reason fled; panic commanded me to run, so I did. Cattails and tall grasses whipped my skin, setting off new panics. Then, suddenly, strong arms caught me, branding me with a hot impression of Emerson's body against mine.

"Stop. Stop!" He turned me around, pushing me to sit on the ground. On his knees in an instant, he pushed my skirts aside.

My chest burned, my heart pounding too hard to be contained, it seemed. My trembling lips parted to babble as I tugged my hems higher. I couldn't see, and I felt so queer— lightheaded and parched. "Am I bleeding? Am I going to die?"

Emerson's hands smoothed over my ankles, along the curve of my calf. At first they searched, their urgency evident, but then . . . they stilled. He stilled. His voice low, he said, "I don't see a thing. You feel all right?"

"I'm not sure; I can't tell," I said, pulling my knees to my chest.

He searched again, fingers whispering across my bare ankles. His breath fell on my skin, heat that thawed the gripping cold within me. Bowing his head, he rested his brow against my knee; his lashes skimmed a subtle touch—and then, his lips. "I think you'll survive."

Something turned—some transient gear, a second's passing that defied time and stretched on—and I slipped my hand into his hair. Twisting his waves around my fingers, I still felt odd, but decidedly more effervescent.

And this switch rendered itself in my voice, rubbing it low and throaty. "I don't think I will."

His hand tightened around my ankle; he surrendered to me a kiss—the tenderest caress against the curve of my knee. And then another, more deliberate.

He lingered there, lips parted, breath hot, before pressing his head against my hand. My blood thundered, and surely, so did his. I felt it, in the trembling of the earth; I saw it in flowers that suddenly blossomed around us. Clean white light spilled over us, a dancing waver of sunbeams reflected off the water.

Raising his eyes to mine, he said nothing. He was wrecked; he was beautiful. And he'd spoken a perfect truth: it wouldn't be the end of the world to guess and get it wrong. There was always the glorious possibility I would get it right. So I leaned over, my thumb trailing the rise of his cheek, and I kissed him.

I claimed him. He was mine.

We lay in the green grass as daylight faded around us.

Perhaps we had been there too long, but it was hard to

imagine shaking myself off and heading back to chores just yet. The restive wind had finally settled, the sky clean of clouds and haze.

Comfortable in the crook of Emerson's arm, I chained hyacinth and indigo into a circlet. It was a silly thing, a childish frippery, but it made me smile to crown him with delicate blue flowers.

He rose, pulling me up to sit with him. Arching a brow, he took the circlet from his head and dropped it onto mine."Prettier on you," he murmured. Then he framed my face with his broad, strong hands and tipped it up for a kiss. He still tasted sweet, of the sand plums he'd coaxed into ripening.

"I don't know; you're terribly pretty," I said, laughing against his lips before melting into them again.

I could have lain there a hundred hours, a hundred days, endlessly mapping his face and his hands. We had not time enough to memorize each other, but we could linger only so much. We both knew it and reluctantly pulled away.

Smoothing my hair, I said, "Where are you going from here, Em?"

"I don't know," he said. He ran his thumbs beneath his suspenders, more, I thought, to soothe himself than to straighten them. Squinting into the distance, he said, "Ireland, maybe."

My throat knotted. Another country? Another world entirely? I managed to say, "Is that so?"

"California," he continued. He reached for me, catching my hand and kissing it roughly. "Paris, France—actually, not Paris, sorry. I don't think we'd mix, me and Paris, do you?"

In spite of myself, I managed to laugh. "If we're being frank with each other, then I'd have to say no. You and the City of Lights seem very ill-suited to one another."

Emerson slid closer to me, wrapping arms around me. He brushed his nose against my temple. "What could you live with?"

"What makes you think I'm coming?"

I meant it only to tease, but my voice broke when I said it, and hot tears stung my eyes. Though I tried to wipe them, he managed first, whispering some nonsense sound meant to comfort me. I composed myself with a breath, so he kissed my brow, then stretched away. His face impossible to read, he thrust a hand into his pocket.

"I lost the chain a while back," he said, taking my hand and pressing something cool into the palm. "It's not a ring, but it's a promise."

Opening my fingers, I gazed at the pendant that lay in my hand. Blue glass glinted in the sunlight, carved into the shape of a teardrop and bound with silver wire. Twisting the delicate lid, I lifted it to my nose. The faintest hint of rose-water wafted up.

"Where did you get this?" I asked, already possessive of it.

"It was my mother's. Like I said, it's a promise." He waited for me to say something, impatiently—I wasn't sure he had patience in him. He closed my fingers around the pendant and said, "Sleep on it."

I took account of myself, and then I kissed the back of his hand. "I came out here ruined. Leaving with you can't possibly ruin me more."

Incredulous, Emerson pressed a finger into my lower lip. "You really are some kind of romantic, you know that?" He hauled himself to his feet, then offered me his hand. "Come on, I'll take you home."

Fat and happy on a day's grazing, Epona barely moved when Emerson mounted her. She gave a careless toss of her head when he pulled me up to sit in front of him. My skirts were filthy, hitched high over my knees—I looked exactly a shameless, ruined thing, and I didn't care.

His strong arms around me, the sweetness of his kiss still on my lips, gold and green streaked by, the prairie turned to an antique sea. My hair whipped around us, our own dark halo as he roughed his cheek against mine.

It seemed like we could ride anywhere—that oceans couldn't keep us from Irish cliffs or Italian shores, from the bells of San Francisco or the revels of New Orleans. In that moment, everything was light.

In the next, it was fire.

Eighteen

At first, the orange light and graying haze seemed like sunset, but it came from the east. An eerie calm accompanied it, winds still, the sky clear. Smoke—not a single point but a wall of it—veiled the horizon. Its sharp scent was a suggestion—like a tickling of the senses, motion caught from the corner of the eye.

Emerson realized it the same time I did. He tightened his arm around my waist as he slowed Epona to a walk. He paced her back and forth, peering into the distance. "Might be they're burning off some brush."

"Wishful thinking," I said. I had no proof of imaginary intentions, but I did have my gift. And there was little water that way, only a few faint points of silver. I looked over my shoulder to tell him that, but the wind kicked up.

It carried fire on it—stoking the one in the distance so that flames, not just smoke, climbed the sky. Delicate ash fluttered around us, dove-gray motes against the unearthly sky.

We took off fast toward Birdie's soddy. Scored by waves of heat, I had the awful luxury of watching the prairie devoured. It was as if someone had traced a thick, soot line in the distance and pushed it ever faster toward us with an infernal breath.

Birdie's voice rent the air. Her voice was ragged with screaming, and as we approached, I realized she was screaming for me. I threw a leg over the saddle, trusting Emerson to drop me safely to my feet. Stumbling when I hit the ground, I found my balance and ran to the front of the yard.

"Birdie! Birdie, I'm here," I said, all but crashing into her.

Furious and relieved, Birdie grabbed my shoulder and shook it. "Where have you been?" Louella clung to her like a little monkey, twisting a loose lock of Birdie's hair in her hand.

"I was with Mr. Birch," I admitted. I said it, and he came around the house, commanding Epona with a firm hand. She stamped at the ground, throwing her head—perhaps realizing better than any of us the danger.

Eyes narrowing, Birdie cut through me with a look. Letting go, she pushed past me and stalked over to Emerson. It surprised me when she untangled Louella's hand from her hair, and thrust her into his arms.

"Take her to Mrs. Herrington at the general."

Louella started to cry. She strained over Emerson's arms, struggling mightily to escape him and return to a familiar embrace. It couldn't have been easy to keep a grip on her, especially with Epona so unsettled, but he managed. He stole but a single look in my direction, a tangling gaze full of fear and reassurance. I pressed my hand to my heart, urging him on with a nod. And with that, he was off, cradling the baby to his chest as he rode hard toward town.

"Get the yoke," Birdie said. She disappeared inside, emerging with her two cook pots. I did as she told me, hanging pails on either end of the yoke, and we hurried to the well, filling all we could before turning back.

Birdie held the pots out wide, trying to keep from spilling even a drop. "Start with the roof."

"What about the chickens?" I asked.

Shaking her head, Birdie stopped and considered the straw slant of the soddy. "If they want to carry a bucket to their coop, they're welcome." Heaving back, Birdie flung the first pot full of water at the house. It splashed low, darkening the soddy walls.

I threw the yoke off, plucking up one of the pails. My aim

was little better. It was only because I had more water to throw that more water landed where we wanted it.

Heat swirled around us. Ash fluttered down, a pale rain that bittered each breath. Birdie's second cast actually splashed across the roof, and the third, which she dipped from my buckets, did as well. I threw the last of that pail after it. Then, in perfect time, we hurried back to the well.

The fire was no longer a distant threat. It was ravenous, swallowing miles of prairie by the minute. It belched blue smoke into the heavens, turning the setting sun into a blood-red disk.

I had no time to wonder what apocalyptic futures might be found in a sunset like that. I had to draw water; I had to burn my hands on rough rope; I had to run.

Tripping on her skirts, Birdie lost her pots to the parched ground. I shucked the yoke off, shoving a pail into her hands. Taking mine up, we threw at once. The roof was parched too — an unrelenting summer had stolen every drop of water it could. The whole world was tinder, and we stood helpless within it.

Again and again, we ran for the well. The fire swept closer, a terrible clock marking time. Now every breath burned. It seared going in and came out on violent coughs. We staggered more; the water hit its mark less.

Emptying her pot, Birdie scrubbed her face with her sleeve, then started for the well again. "Come on!"

"No, no, Birdie, wait." I grabbed her wrist, pulling her back. I felt disconnected, my thoughts swirling in a light-headed distance. But even I could see that the flames had come too close to risk another run to the well. "It's too close. It's too close. What do we do?"

Birdie's breath whistled. She looked behind us, then back at the fire. "I don't know. Let's go lie down. It's cooler inside."

Both our senses had fled, it seemed. The soddy was nothing more than an earth-brick oven. Even if the roof held— especially if it held—we would die in it. Trying to stay my aunt and reason through an inferno, I suddenly laughed.

It was a bitter, ridiculous sound, more a bark than anything else. After the year I spent in crêpe and gauze, courting Death and praying for his coming—he had finally arrived, and I wanted nothing to do with him.

Then, in the swirling heat, a chill crossed my skin. As the blaze swept toward us, I realized I drowned in fire here. I drowned in it, and the sky was wide as the sea.

"Don't move," I ordered Birdie.

I stepped away from her, isolating myself in the smoky yard. No more did I feel the heat the wind carried from the fire. The fire had come; it threw furious sparks at the sky. Embers fell on me now, ashes to be.

So I reached down, toward the heartbeat beneath earth and stone. And I reached up, drawn by the faint pulse in darkening clouds. There was no one to dig, no intermediary to bring the water forth. I would do it, or we would die.

The whole of my life was supposed to show itself to me, but it didn't. I felt no looming calm. What kind of end was this? How dare God or the fates or the *elements* abandon us like this? The last of my breath twisted into a scream. It was a furious sound—no mourning banshee, I screamed until I tasted iron in my mouth.

Something struck me; it was like a hammer to the head. I collapsed to my knees, falling into the dirt. None of my thoughts would order themselves. I saw a ship in the clouds; I tasted roasted meat. And I burned from the inside—burned as if I'd swallowed coals.

It was a feast day, I thought, and something ran over me. Little birds or spiders, everywhere, plucking at my skin. Twitching there, I reached for the fairy lights that crossed my gaze. They flickered and flickered; my fingers spasmed of their own accord—they caught nothing.

It began to rain.

I flew, through a sandstorm, on a long gold ribbon. An eerie chorus played around me, disconnected voices that sounded miles away or right inside my head: *birch rode the baby's safe house on fire was lightning.* The odd hymn leapt and jumped; I couldn't catch its melody or meaning.

My head was too heavy for my neck, it seemed. Uncoordinated, my eyes opened independently, one, then the other, the world swimming around me in strange, hazy shapes. A flash of green eye, a spark of rose-patterned blue —

Then, suddenly, some band within me snapped. It jolted me into my skin again. In one moment, I had floated unaware — now I felt every jounce of the road. A needlefall of raindrops stung my face, and I raised a hand to fend them off.

"Be still," Birdie said. She curled her arms around me, and I realized my head lay in her lap, as if I were a babe. Tugging a quilt around me, she shielded most of me from the storm. "We're almost to town."

"A few minutes at best," Theo said.

I lifted my head when I heard his voice. My thoughts ordered and disordered themselves, but I managed to piece together my surroundings. Red velvet, blue calico — Theo's phaeton, Birdie's nine-patch quilt. We rode into town; the sky cracked with lightning, warned with thunder.

I had to find my mouth with my fingers; once I had, I asked, "Did the house burn?"

Exhaling a weary laugh, Birdie pulled the quilt tighter around me. "No, duck."

"But the house didn't burn?" I asked. I had a feeling I'd already asked it, but I couldn't remember the answer.

Face pinched, Birdie said, "The house is fine; now, be still. You can talk your head off after Doc Julian looks you over." And then, to effect the stillness she commanded, she pulled a corner of the quilt over my face. My lashes fluttered against the patches, but the darkness invited me down so pleasantly, I couldn't resist it.

Between blinks, I dozed, and in a flip-book second, town appeared around us. In the next, Theo gathered me; another flash, and I found myself handed into new arms.

They carried me inside, into a building fresh with the scent of menthol, tangy with the bite of an iron stove nice and hot. The air was thick with water, pleasant humidity laced with camphor to settle the senses.

"All right, let's take a look," an unfamiliar man said. He peeled my layers, raising my face to his. He washed with lye soap—his hands were rough with it, though his touch was gentle.

Birdie appeared from nowhere to take my hand. "Lightning struck her; I thought she was dead at first. She was insensible for most of the drive and just started to come round."

"Did the house burn?" I asked.

No one answered, and the doctor grew rather more insistent in his examination. Pulling the quilt open, he murmured in surprise. My day gown was in rags, at least along my left side. With some detached amazement, I marveled at the char that was my bared shoulder. It matched the sole of my foot, and I wondered where my shoes were.

"She seems intact physically," the doctor said. He picked up a little mirror to flash in my eyes.

My ears rang, but each flash recalled the one that had addled me so completely. As I lay blanketed in pleasant humidity, the doctor bade me follow his finger.

"What's your name?" he asked pleasantly, and I told him. "Good. Can you say your ABCs?"

Furrowing my brow, I searched for the first letter a long time. When the A finally floated to the surface, I rattled the whole twenty-six easily. With each test, I came back to myself. So much so that when the doctor thrust his thick fingers into my mouth without warning, I slapped them.

"Zora!" Birdie exclaimed.

My face flushed. "I'm sorry; you surprised me."

The pinhole width of my world widened. Birdie sat beside me; Dr. Julian leaned back on his stool, fortunately for me, half-smiling. Medical diagrams covered the walls; the camphor burner sputtered a bit.

Light glinted off the sheen of Dr. Julian's skin as he put his tools aside. Rubbing his hands dry on a towel, he seemed to mull over his diagnosis a moment, then finally said, "Well, Mrs. Neal, I'd say she's going to be just fine. She might be discomposed for a spell, but nothing lasting, I don't think. Bring her back if you're concerned, and stop by in an hour or two. I'll mix a salve for those burns."

"Thank you, Dr. Julian," Birdie said. She had tears in her voice, but she swallowed them. "What a lucky girl."

"Or unlucky," the doctor joked.

But sitting there among them, I felt neither lucky nor unlucky. I was simply myself—Zora Stewart, late of Oklahoma Territory—the springsweet and now rainmaker. Shuddering, I pulled the quilt around my shoulders modestly. Never again a rainmaker, I decided. I was no god; my gift had limits.

Birdie helped me up; I felt odd, as if my feet didn't quite touch the ground. But with her arm around my shoulder, I could totter along. The cooler air outside was a blessed relief, rain still a mist in the air. The road that ran through West Glory was a creek at the moment, so Birdie led me the long way around to the hotel.

Just before we went inside, I frowned. "Birdie?"

"Watch your step," Birdie said. "What?"

I remembered a fire; I still tasted smoke. Pushing sodden hair out of my face, I asked her quietly, "Did the house burn?"

"No, duck." The worried lines on her brow deepened. But patiently, she tightened the quilt around my shoulders, then led me inside.

~~~~~~~

The hotel was our home for the moment. It had been a few days, though how many exactly I couldn't count. We had to wait for the rain to stop and the smoke to clear—and, though it was unspoken, for me to recover enough of my wits that Birdie wouldn't go mad tending me on her own.

It was strange to sit between walls so thin. I heard conversations on the other side, as if they were whispered directly into my ears.

The rain had quenched most of the fire. The single line that had swept on toward town was drowned by a makeshift brigade of firefighters—mostly cowboys on rest and the shopkeepers who peopled West Glory by day and night.

The Baders had lost their new barn and most of their livestock; Jim Polley's back forty had burned, leaving him with half as much crop as he'd expected for the year.

No one had died—everyone said this in hushed, reverent tones. I had yet to witness the tornados and the dust storms, the grasshopper legions and the droughts that this land apparently boasted on dark occasion.

People found death an unfriendly neighbor here, sadly regular, reluctantly expected as the price of living far from the bounds of a city. To believe it a miracle when all managed to breathe another day—it was more cynical than I could bear.

The sitting room door opened, and I groaned inwardly when I heard Birdie greeting Theo and Mrs. Herrington. We'd had a steady stream of callers—Birdie's friends, of course, but curiosity seekers as well. They wanted to get a glimpse of the girl who'd called down lightning.

None of them were Emerson—I wondered about him, for I had last seen him carrying the baby away on horseback. I thought it possible he'd delivered her and ridden on—to find some impossible piece of land that was his alone. It was a naïve, reckless fear—but after all my reason and rationale, it seemed I wasn't entirely immune to lovesickness.

Theo's voice interrupted my thoughts. "Have you talked to her, Birdie?"

I arched a brow. Since when did Theo call my aunt by her given name? Turning away from the window, I crept to the door to listen more deliberately. Some of the conversation was hard to make out, because Mrs. Herrington had decided to play with Louella.

"Riding a horsey, riding to town," Mrs. Herrington sang. Her heel thumped on the floor—no doubt she dandled Louella on her knee. "Riding a horsey, don't fall down!"

Between that, I caught a snatch of Birdie's reply, ". . . just need to be certain she knows what I'm telling her."

Theo hummed thoughtfully. "Is she still asking if the house burned?"

"Riding a horsey!" Louella cried, so I didn't hear the answer. It piqued my curiosity, because now I desperately wanted to know: how many times had I asked? And had it? I almost opened the door to inquire; I was glad, in the next moment, that I hadn't.

". . . you come courting, I'm sure she'll understand."

"I don't want to give the impression that I'm inconstant . . ."

Laughing, Birdie said, "I've got news for you, Theo—I don't give a tinker's damn what people think about me or you."

Mrs. Herrington crowed, "Don't fall down!"

My head hurt, and I pulled my wrapper on. My thoughts were not so quick as before, but if I rubbed my temples, I could sort them out well enough. The bare slips of conversation I'd overheard didn't make sense if Theo meant to try to court me again. But if he meant to call on Birdie . . .

I covered my smiling mouth with my hand. And then I shivered, for I felt a familiar tremor run through me. My heart jumped up, my blood running fast with anticipation. He hadn't gone; he'd come for me.

The tremor was distant, struggling through planks and nails to reach me, so I rushed to the window to look out.

Through the gray cloud of rain, I saw Emerson hitching his horse across the street. Throwing the sash up, I leaned out and waved to catch his eye. He turned, as if he'd known exactly where to seek me, then ducked his head as he started across the street.

Instead of coming through the hotel's foyer, he stood at the edge of the porch and called up. "Hold this for me, Zo."

I was confused, until he threw his hat for me to catch. I managed, just barely, and the mad fool grabbed the porch roof and hefted himself up. In spite of inclement weather and all good senses, he scrambled up the slope toward me.

Catching the windowsill with one hand, he leaned in to kiss me hard before reclaiming his hat. His lips were cold from riding but tasted sweet with rain. We were bright and alive, a two-penny imitation of Romeo and Juliet, but I had no plans to say goodbye, and I felt certain he would not end up drinking poison from my lips.

Giddy, I clasped his face and kissed his brow, his cheek. Before he could speak, I pulled him in again, tasting his mouth once more before murmuring into it, "You don't care at all that I'm ruined."

"Not a bit," he answered.

From behind me, Birdie cleared her throat. "Well, I do. You get down right now and come to the door like your mama raised you decent, Mr. Birch."

Nineteen

"Where will you be going?" Birdie demanded.

I think she simply needed to assert her authority one last time. That I had buttoned my shoes and pulled my wrapper around my shoulders told her I intended to go.

Emerson stood at the door, not because he hadn't been invited in—he had—but because Louella had burst into tears the moment she saw him. Whatever memory she might have had of his magic had been erased by a terrifying ride through fire.

Fussing sweetly, Mrs. Herrington had carried Louella into the bedroom to soothe her, but still Emerson ventured no farther inside.

Blessedly, Theo had excused himself, claiming he would fetch lemonade for the ladies. From the length of time he'd been gone, it seemed he had caught a train south to harvest the lemons himself.

And who could blame him? Even if he *had* decided to court Birdie, he had a heart, still recently trampled. I could hardly hold it against him, finding a long errand to run.

Slipping my hand into my pocket, I fingered the warped glass of Emerson's pendant. The lightning had transformed it, too. What was once a bottle was now a sealed, elongated tear. I worried it with my fingers, trying to find an answer to Birdie's question—but in the end, I didn't have one.

Since I said nothing, Birdie cut Emerson a look. He would take the blame, whether he deserved it or not. "Well?"

Emerson finally said, "We haven't decided yet."

Huffing, Birdie caught me by the shoulders, fixing my wrap. "I can see the telegrams now. Pauline shouting down the wires at me—*You let my addlepated daughter run off with a sooner, and you don't know where they're headed?* That's some position to put your poor aunt in."

"You don't have to tell her anything. I'll write as soon as we light somewhere," I promised.

"I've never been to Baltimore," Emerson offered.

Birdie turned on him, hands on hips, surveying him with her glass-green eyes. "And you'd best not set foot in it until there's a ring on her finger."

Blushing, I murmured, "Birdie, please."

"Her father's a lawyer," Birdie told Emerson. Her eyes widened with a wicked glint, and she went on. "And her mother's a dragon. I hope that hide of yours is thick, boy."

Certain now that I would be leaving with him, Emerson dared a smile. "That's a lie, Mrs. Neal. You hope they'll split me like a game hen, but I appreciate the sentiment all the same."

Wonder of wonders, Birdie laughed. But she didn't embrace him—it wasn't her way. What she owed him for carrying Louella away from the fire she'd repaid by letting me go. There would be no fondness between them.

In fact, when I embraced her, she whispered into my ear, "Keep the well money in case you need a ticket away from him."

I kissed Birdie and stole into the bedroom to kiss Louella goodbye too. I wondered if I would be a faint memory for her or if I would disappear from her thoughts entirely once I was gone from her sight. Picking her up, I buried my face against her curls one last time, breathing in her baby sweetness.

"Don't punch any chickens while I'm gone," I told her.

She smiled sleepily as I returned her to Mrs. Herrington's arms. "You hit the birdie."

"I certainly did," I told her.

Then I slipped away, with one more kiss for my aunt, one

more look back to catch a glimpse of Lou's round little face. Without much notice, we slipped down the stairs and outside, where the rain had finally stopped.

Looking back at the hotel, I caught sight of Theo in the window. He dipped his head, as if trying to make me out for certain. And then he smiled gently, raising a hand in farewell. I waved back, and the tightness in my chest from doing him so badly dissipated at last.

This place, I realized as Emerson pulled me onto Epona, I wouldn't miss at all. For all the bright moments, for the rain-washed skies and the golden wave of grasses that flowed across the land — for the satisfaction in learning to wrest a life from hard, dry earth — this was no place for me.

As we passed out of town limits, I counted the homesteader stakes that marked each plot — and I couldn't help but wonder who had peopled these acres before the government had cut it into parcel prizes.

For the moment, it was a black, stubbled field. Smoke no longer rose, but it was clear where the fire had stopped — and how far it had reached. The ground shone like fired clay. All that remained was ash.

Though I wouldn't miss this place, I would miss the people all my days. Leaning against Emerson, I rested my temple against his jaw and said, "Could we stop at Birdie's for my things?"

"Already did," he said. He looked down at me, tightening his arm around my waist. "She knew I was coming for you. She told me what to pack."

My throat tightened. "I had a memento . . ."

"Your dance card?" He kissed my hair, urging Epona on a little faster. "I've got it. Couple of dresses, a sampler you did with Louella. Some mail, too. Is there something else?"

Relief spilled over me, and I pulled his hand up to keep and clutch between mine. Thomas had nothing to say now; my love for him was pure and true, and it remained within me yet.

That was a memento too—something precious to remember, even as I looked forward to a future at Emerson's side. I kissed his fingertips and murmured my thanks against them.

"No, that's everything. Thank you."

I was then content to ride off in his arms. To drive on toward our future. But the Territories, as I previously noted, were hard, and though I thought they would let me slip away in a gentle embrace, I was most assuredly mistaken.

<hr />

"Whose horse is that?" I asked when Emerson's cabin came into view.

Wandering the ruined yard, a white horse searched for something to graze. The fire had, perversely, preserved the cabin's walls and its windows but swallowed the roof whole.

None of his garden remained, nor his lean-to. His buckboard was there but a cindered mess. The fire had swept through so voraciously, it devoured every bit of wood from it, leaving only the iron frame and trappings.

Shaking his head, Emerson slowed. Tension ran through him; I felt him tighten everywhere. "Not sure." I could tell he wanted to follow that with a *You stay here,* but two in a saddle was an ungainly thing. He had to let me down first so he could follow.

"I'll be right back," he said, putting my hand on Epona's flank.

I was still unsteady on my feet, and though I was clear-headed enough to *want* to defy him, I was likewise sensible enough to refuse the urge. There was nothing gained in being contrary for contrary's sake. "I'll be right here."

Emerson headed inside, and I turned to take in the enormity of the fire around me. My nose stung a bit—the rain had pounded away the smoke, but wet remains had their own acid to them. After all, we made lye for our soap from water and wood ash.

Smoothing my skirts, I sighed at the senselessness of it. A

whole prairie gone in one night. And yet, among the ashes, I noted the smallest of green shoots. The white horse had found them easily—unconcerned with what it all meant.

I started at a sudden crack. Jerking my head up, I saw motion in one of the windows, and glass glinting as it rained to the ground. Sharp voices rose up. I couldn't make them out, but I didn't need to.

They were angry; I was afraid. In spite of the trembling set loose in me, I ran to the house.

Though I hurried, I felt the world temper its pace. At the door, I took in the tableau in an instant. Emerson locked in struggle with a blond man. Broken glass. A ransacked cabin.

It was ruined. Soot coated every surface but the table. A leather bag lay open there, stuffed with a lantern, a few books, and a knife. I recognized the knife; I'd taken it once from Emerson, to clean rabbits for stew.

I caught a glimpse of Emerson's face as he twisted and then . . . Royal Wakes'. My fear turned to fury. Robbing coaches wasn't enough for him. The coward had resorted to looting after a disaster.

They crashed into one of the walls. It threatened with a groan. A trickle of blood ran down Emerson's face. Royal struck again, the awful sound of flesh colliding with flesh too visceral and real.

I could take up the knife — I could. I screamed when they crashed into the opposite wall. Their bodies flowed together, one muslin shirt very much like another. I would never forgive myself if I stuck a blade into the wrong flesh. In truth, I wasn't sure I could forgive myself if I stuck it in the right flesh, either.

In a panic, I spun around, looking for something — anything — and then I saw it. Emerson's rifle lay in the soot, barely visible. I snatched it up by the barrel.

When I had a clear shot, I brought the stock down on Royal's head. A sickening crack filled the air. He dropped to the ground. Ash and dust puffed around him, stirred by his breath. But he moved not at all — he'd been a puppet, and I'd cut his strings.

Emerson stood there, mute in his surprise. I threw the rifle down and grabbed the bag from the table. "Come on! Come on!"

Coming around, Emerson snatched up the rifle and followed me outside. He dashed straight for Epona. It took but one step into the stirrup and he threw his leg over, the motion easy. Turning her around, he reached for me, but I brushed past.

Catching the white horse by its reins, I pulled myself up. I was a graceless, lumbering thing compared with the way

Emerson handled a horse, but I managed all the same. Taking reins in hand, I geed the horse.

She was an arrow, flying fast and straight. It took only the gentlest touch to command her. I'm not sure how far we ran, but with every pounding step, my fear peeled away. Hesitation rattled from my bones; I made my own thunder. I was new and vibrant, drunk with audacity.

Epona caught up quickly, her hooves rumbling across the earth. Emerson had to raise his voice to be heard over our flight. "I thought you didn't handle arms!"

"That's hardly what I did," I called back.

"Now who's quibbling? Do you know what they do with horse thieves?"

"I have no idea!" I laughed, casting an irrepressible smile in his direction. "I don't plan to find out!"

Raising my face to the sun, I pulled off my bonnet and let the wind take my hair. The prairie blurred around us, a streak left in our wake. Kissed by sunlight and warmth, by everything possible, I whooped and sat high in my saddle.

I was alive, and I *wanted* to be alive until my time.

Epilogue

The end I'd expected in the West was a beginning after all.
It was not until Emerson and I stopped for the night that I
discovered how much of one.

Rifling through the mail in Emerson's saddlebag, I read
missives from Mama and Papa and a few pretty notes from
Mattie. They seemed so far away, hints of their perfumes
and colognes on the pages. They were little scraps of Baltimore to tease my senses — but they no longer made me ache;
I didn't yearn for that city by the bay.

Kissing Mama's letter, I tucked it away with the rest.
Then I reached for the remaining envelope.

A chill came on fast when I saw the handwriting. It had
once graced a hundred futures at the last slant of daylight.

But that was impossible—it couldn't possibly be true. The letter inside illuminated nothing, it simply said:

Please come.

"Emerson," I said when I finally found my breath. Folding the letter in half, I looked to him. He was already drowsy, resting his head against the saddlebags and trying to fall asleep.

"Mmm?"

Rubbing a hand down his face, he held out a hand to me, beckoning me. His face was soft, clean now that we'd washed in a river, and unlined as he invited slumber. He was handsome and unmarred, and I wondered very much if I would trouble his brow if I spoke. I spoke nonetheless.

"I want to go to Chicago. Just for a little while."

When I leaned in, he took advantage. Pulling me to lie in his arms, he fixed me against his side and kissed my temple. The raw, rich scent of his skin surrounded me; his warmth lured like a siren to close my eyes and sleep awhile as well.

I pressed my knuckle into his ribs; not hard, just enough to get his attention. "Chicago, Em?"

"Whatever makes you happy, Zo."

He smiled, and didn't bother to ask why. And I was glad. There would be no explaining that I needed to see, with my own eyes, a dark miracle—

Amelia van den Broek, risen from the dead.

Acknowledgments

$\mathbf{M}$any thanks to . . .

My editor, Julie Tibbott, for taking the chance on these wild, elemental children — her support and enthusiasm have lent more magic to *The Springsweet* than she knows.

Jennifer LaBracio, for all the marketing you can shake a stick at; Jennifer Groves, my very own publicity star, and the entire team at Houghton Mifflin Harcourt for turning words into beautiful, beautiful books.

My agent Jim McCarthy, for notes, for plans, and for those brilliant e-mails that neutralize my neuroses in a single blow.

Darlene Engleking from Engleking's Country Beef Shop, for selling me her gorgeous farm eggs and patiently answering questions about them as well.

Leah Hansen from Hansen Wagon and Wheel, for the detailed explanation of buckboards and how to attach them to horses.

Carrie Ryan, for keeping me sane when I most assuredly was not sane myself and knowing exactly when to make me cry.

Aprilynne Pike, the amazing, incredible, iPhone-at-the-gym-reading genius. I owe you at least 1/28th of my soul.

Sarah MacLean, for indulging me even when I horrify her, and R. J. Anderson, for laughing when I try not to horrify her.

Sarah Rees Brennan, my Sass Sr., who tells me books and movies, and pets my head, and quite possibly never sleeps.

Cheryl Renée Herbsman, for reading blind; Sarah Cross, for forgiving me Thomas; Sonia Gensler, for checking my Okie; Christine Johnson for telling me it wasn't the worst book in the world.

Rachel Hawkins, who I hope will now forgive me for whiffing the amazeballs in Decatur.

L. K. Madigan, for reading everything first; for the great emptiness I feel knowing that this was our last.

My Wendi, because she loves Zora the most (and me, too).

My Jason, for every sacrifice he's made for me and for our family—you are a good, good man.